What happens in Vegas . . .

It was her skin that Reed loved the most. The cheap hotel sheets were scratchy, but her pale, creamy skin was unbelievably soft and smooth, as if it had never been exposed to the outside world. . . .

"Do you . . . do you want to?" she whispered suddenly, her eyes still closed.

"Want to what?" He kissed her cheek, then her forehead, her nose, and, finally, her lips.

"You know." She opened her eyes. A tear was pooling in one of the corners. "I don't know if you brought . . . protection." It sounded like she had to choke the word out. "But if you did, maybe we should—"

Reed rolled off of her and propped himself up on his side. "Where's this coming from?"

Beth tucked a strand of hair behind her ear and, instead of turning to face him, stayed on her back, staring up at the cracked ceiling. "I know I said I didn't want to, not yet, but that was before . . . You're just really good to me, and I thought—I want to make you happy."

"You thought *this* would make me happy?" he asked incredulously, his voice rising. "You doing this as if—as if you owe me something? Do you think I'm that kind of guy? . . . Why would you think . . . I told you I'd wait. I told you I didn't care."

"I know. But . . ."

She didn't need to say it out loud. He got it: She hadn't believed him.

"Why now?" he asked. "Why tonight?"

At first she didn't answer, and when she finally did her voice was almost too soft to hear.

"Because I don't deserve you."

SEVEN DEADLY SINS

Lust
Envy
Pride
Wrath
Sloth
Gluttony

SOON TO BE COMMITTED:
Greed

SEVEN DEADLY SINS

Gluttony

ROBIN WASSERMAN

SIMON PULSE

New York   London   Toronto   Sydney

SIMON PULSE
An imprint of Simon & Schuster Children's Publishing Division
1230 Avenue of the Americas, New York, NY 10020
Copyright © 2007 by Robin Wasserman
All rights reserved, including the right of reproduction in whole or in part in any form.
SIMON PULSE and colophon are registered trademarks of Simon & Schuster, Inc.
Designed by Ann Zeak
The text of this book was set in Bembo.
Manufactured in the United States of America
First Simon Pulse edition March 2007
10 9 8 7
Library of Congress Control Number 2006933723
ISBN-13: 978-1-4169-0719-0
ISBN-10: 1-4169-0719-X

For Richard, David, and Natalie Roher

And for Aunt Susan, who has heard it all—

and is always willing to listen

They are as sick that surfeit
with too much as they that starve with nothing.
—William Shakespeare, *The Merchant of Venice*

I eat too much
I drink too much
I want too much
Too much
—Dave Matthews Band, "Too Much"

chapter

1

"Anything worth doing," Kane Geary intoned, gulping down a glowing green shot that looked radioactive, "is worth overdoing."

"Thanks for the wisdom, O Wise One." Adam Morgan pressed his hands together and gave Kane an exaggerated bow. "What did I ever do without you to guide me through the mysteries of the universe?"

"Less sarcasm." Kane clinked his shot glass against the half-full pitcher of beer. "More drinking."

It was nearly midnight, and the bar was packed. To their left, a whale-size cowboy in a ten-gallon hat tucked hundred-dollar bills down the cleavage of a harem of spangled showgirls half his age. Against the back wall, a table of white-jumpsuit-clad Elvis impersonators argued loudly about whether *The Ed Sullivan Show* hip swivel properly began with a swing to the left or the right. The bartender, who wore a gold bikini and a cupcake-size hair bun over each ear, would have been the spitting image of Princess

Leia—were he not a man. The walls were lined with red velvet and the ceiling covered with mirrors.

Welcome to Vegas.

Adam felt like he'd set foot on an alien planet; Kane, on the other hand, had obviously come home.

"Where do you think Harper and Miranda are?" Adam asked, nursing his beer.

Kane rolled his eyes and spread his arms wide. "Morgan. Dude. Focus. Look around you. This is nirvana. Who the hell cares where the girls are?"

"If they got stuck somewhere—"

"They'll be fine. You're the one I'm worried about." Kane clapped him on the back. "You need another drink, kid. You've got to loosen up."

Adam shook his head. "No more. It's late. And I'm—"

"Lame. Very lame." Kane grabbed Adam's glass and downed the remaining beer in a single gulp. Then he filled it back up to the brim and slammed it down in front of Adam. "But we'll fix that."

"Oh, will we?" Adam asked dryly.

"Adam, my doubting disciple, if there's one thing you learn from me tonight, let it be this." He was silent for a long moment, and Adam began to wonder whether all that beer sloshing around in his brain had swept away his train of thought.

"Yes?" Adam finally said.

Kane leaned across the table, the better to wheeze his sour breath into Adam's face. "This is Vegas, baby." His voice was hushed, almost reverential. "America's Playground. City of Lights. Sin City." He leaned in even closer, as if to whisper a crucial secret. *"This is Vegas, baby!"* Adam recoiled as Kane let loose an ear-piercing whoop of elation. "Live it up!"

"This is definitely *not* Vegas," Harper Grace observed sourly.

Miranda Stevens pulled the car over to the side of the road and shut off the ignition. "Thanks for the news flash," she snapped. "If you hadn't pointed that out, I might have mistaken that"—she gestured toward the hulking mound of rock and dirt jutting out of the desert landscape—"for the Trump Taj Mahal."

"That's in Atlantic City," Harper corrected her.

"Gosh, maybe *that's* where we are," Miranda said in mock revelation. "I knew we shouldn't have taken that left turn. . . ."

Harper tore open a bag of Doritos and kicked her feet up onto the dashboard. "I really hope that's not sarcasm," she said, neglecting to offer Miranda a chip. "Because the person responsible for stranding us here in the middle of East Bumblefuck should probably steer clear of the sarcasm right about now."

Miranda snatched the bag out of Harper's hands, though it was several hours too late to prevent an explosion of orange crumbs all over the front seat of her precious Honda Civic. "And by the person responsible, I assume you're referring to . . . you?"

Harper raised an eyebrow. "Am *I* driving?"

Harper, doing her share of the work? Miranda snorted at the thought of it. "No, of course not. You're just sitting there innocently, with no responsibilities whatsoever, except, oh . . . *reading the map.*"

That shut her up. Miranda's lips curled up in triumph.

Beating Harper in an argument was a rare victory, one that she planned to savor, lost in the wilderness or not.

"Okay, let's not panic," Harper finally said, a new, ingratiating tone in her voice. "Look on the bright side. It's your birthday—"

"Not for another twenty-four hours," Miranda corrected her.

"We're bound for Vegas," Harper continued.

"Maybe. *Someday.*"

"And we're not stranded," Harper added, grabbing a map off the floor, seemingly at random, "just—"

"Lost.

"Detoured." Harper spread the map across her lap and began tracing out their route with a perfectly manicured pinkie. "We just need to get back to the main highway," she mumbled, "and if we turn back here and cross over Route 161 . . ."

Miranda sighed and tuned her out, resolving to backtrack to the nearest gas station and get directions from a professional. Professional lukewarm coffee dispenser and stale-candy-bar salesman, maybe, but anything would be better than Harper's geographically challenged attempts to guide them. Especially since Harper periodically forgot whether they should be heading east or west.

This was supposed to be a bonding weekend—or, rather, a *re*-bonding weekend, given all the tension of the last few months. But it turned out that five hours in a car together didn't exactly make for a BFF bonanza.

Call it the sisterhood of the traveling crankypants.

Miranda turned the key in the ignition, eager to start driving again—somewhere. Anywhere.

A small, suspicious, gurgling sound issued from the motor. Miranda turned the key again. Nothing. With a sinking feeling, she lowered her eyes to the dashboard indicators: specifically, the gas gauge.

Uh-oh.

"Harper?" she said softly, nibbling at the edge of her lower lip.

"Maybe if we circle around to Route 17," Harper muttered, lost in her own cartographic world. "Or if we—wait, am I looking at this upside down?"

"Harper?" A little louder this time.

"Fine, *you* look at it," Harper said in disgust, pushing the wad of paper off her lap. "And if you tell me one more time that I don't know how to read a map, I'm going to scream. It's not like I didn't—"

"Harper!"

"What?"

Miranda tore the keys out of the ignition and threw them down on the dash, then leaned her head back against the seat. She closed her eyes. "We're out of gas."

She couldn't see the look on Harper's face. But she could imagine it.

There was a long pause. "So you're telling me—" Harper stopped herself, and Miranda could hear her take a deep breath. Her voice got slightly—very slightly—calmer. "You're telling me that we're out of gas. We're out here in the middle of nowhere, and now we're not just lost—"

"We're stranded," Miranda confirmed. "So, Ms. Look On the Bright Side . . . *now* can we panic?"

❖❖❖

He woke her with a kiss.

"Whuh? Where . . . ?" Beth Manning opened her eyes, disoriented and unsure why she was sleeping sitting up, lodged into the corner of a van that stunk of pot and sweat socks. But she smiled, nonetheless. It didn't really matter where she was, or how much her neck and back ached—not when Reed Sawyer's chocolate brown eyes were so close and his dark, curly hair was brushing her skin.

It was the best kind of alarm clock.

"Was I sleeping?" she mumbled, slowly making sense of her surroundings. She remembered piling into the van, nestling into a space between the guitar cases and the drum that was just big enough for one—or two, if they sat nearly on top of each other. She had curled under Reed's arm, leaned her head on his shoulder, promised to stay awake for the long drive, and then zoned out, staring at the grayish brown monotony of the landscape speeding by. "Sorry, I guess I must have drifted off."

"No worries," Reed assured her, giving her another quick peck on the lips. "It was cute."

"Yeah, the snoring was adorable!" Hale called from the driver's seat.

That's right, we're not alone, Beth reminded herself. When Reed was around, it seemed like the rest of the world fell away. But in reality, his bandmates, Fish and Hale, were never far behind. Not that Beth was complaining. She was in no position to complain about anything.

"And the drooling," Fish added teasingly. "The drooling was *especially* attractive."

"I did not drool!" Beth cried indignantly.

"Oh, don't worry." Fish, riding shotgun, twisted

around toward the back and brandished his cell phone. "We've got pictures."

"Shut up, losers," Reed snapped. But Beth just smiled, and snuggled into his side, resting her head in the warm and familiar nook between his chest and shoulder. He looped his arm around her and began lightly tracing out patterns on her arm. She shivered.

Without warning, the van made a sharp left turn, veering into a parking lot and screeching to a stop. "Welcome to Vegas, kids," Hale said, with a sharp blast on the horn. "Gateway to stardom."

Stardom couldn't come soon enough, if it would mean an entourage to carry all the instruments and equipment up to the room. Or, even better, a van with a real lock on the doors that would keep out any thieves desperate enough to steal fifteen-year-old half-busted amplifiers. But since they currently had neither roadies nor locking doors, the three members of the Blind Monkeys had to make due with what they had: the combined strength of three scrawny potheads.

And one ever-faithful blond groupie.

"You don't have to help," Reed told her, pulling his guitar case out of the back. Beth was loaded up like a pack-horse with heavy, scuffed-up duffel bags—no one trusted her to carry the real equipment. "You can go check in and we'll meet you inside."

"I'm fine," she protested, ignoring the way the straps dug into her bare shoulder. "I want to help." She was afraid that if she didn't make herself useful, the other guys might realize that she didn't really belong. Reed might finally figure it out himself.

Yes, she was the one who'd found out about that weekend's All-American Band Battle, and she was the one who'd convinced Reed and the guys to enter. But no matter how much she hung out with them, she'd never be one of them, not really.

And she dreaded the day they got sick of her and left her behind.

Alone.

She couldn't stand that. Not again.

Reed shrugged. "Whatever." He slung his guitar case over his shoulder and hoisted an amp, heading across the parking lot. Beth began to follow, but then, as the hotel rose into full view, she stopped. And gasped.

The Camelot was the cheapest hotel almost-but-not-quite-on the Strip; Beth, a Vegas virgin, would have been willing to bet it was also the gaudiest. The gleaming white monstrosity towered over the parking lot—literally, as its twenty stories were sculpted into the guise of a medieval tower, complete with ramparts, turrets and, down below, a churning, brownish moat. It reminded Beth of a model castle her fourth-grade class had once built from sugar cubes, except that in this version, the royal crest was outlined in neon and featured a ten-foot-tall fluorescent princess wearing a jeweled crown—and little else.

Then there was the piéce de résistance, guarding the palace doors. Beth goggled at the enormous, green animatronic dragon swinging its long neck up and down with an alarmingly loud creak each time it shifted direction. Periodically a puff of smoke would issue from its squarish mouth, followed by a warning siren, and then—

WHOOOSH! A flume of fire blasted out of the dragon,

a jolt of orange and red billowing several feet out into the night. Beth cringed, imagining she could feel the heat.

"It's not going to eat you," Reed teased, tipping his head toward the front doors, which were now nearly eclipsed by smoke. "Let's make a run for it."

Weighed down by luggage and guitars, it wasn't much of a run, but they eventually made it inside the hotel and up to the room. The Camelot had obviously burned through its decorating budget before furnishing the guest rooms, and the Blind Monkeys had reserved the cheapest one available. It smelled like cigarettes, the toilet was clogged, and the tiny window faced a cement airshaft.

There was one bed.

Harper could barely keep her eyes open, but she wasn't about to fall asleep, not when the skeezy tow-truck driver kept sneaking glances at her cleavage. He'd already offered—twice—to bundle her up in one of his ratty old blankets to protect her from the cold. As if she needed some middle-aged dirt-bucket to tuck her in—as if, in fact, she'd be willing to touch anything in this trash heap on wheels. Touching the seat was bad enough; these pants would need to be burned.

Miranda, on the other hand, apparently had no such qualms. She was totally conked out, her head resting on Harper's shoulder. All that complaining—Stop spilling crumbs in the car! Stop sticking your head out the window! Stop flashing the other drivers!—must have worn her out. Or maybe it was just the hour they'd spent shivering in the darkness, waiting for someone to pass by. With no cell reception and no idea how far they were from civilization, they'd been forced to flag down a trucker, crossing their fingers that he wasn't a deranged ax murderer trolling the roads for pretty girls too stupid to fill their gas tanks.

Trucker Hank offered them a ride, and got a quick thanks but no thanks for his trouble. They may have been stupid, but not that stupid. So instead, the guy promised to check in at the next gas station he passed and send someone back to help them.

"We're going to be out here all night," Miranda had moaned, once the truck's lights had disappeared into the distance.

In fact, it had only been another hour, but that had been long enough. When Leroy had finally arrived with his tow truck, offering to take them and their wounded Civic back to "town," they'd climbed in eagerly, only later realizing that the cab of the truck smelled like roadkill, as did Leroy.

It was a long drive.

"Here we are, gals," he said finally, pulling into a tiny, one-pump gas station that looked like a relic from the stone age—or, at least, the fifties. (Same difference.) Harper poked Miranda to wake her up, and climbed out of the truck, sucking in a deep lungful of the fresh air. She'd been hoping to grab something to eat once they got into town, but . . .

"Where is 'here,' exactly?" she asked dubiously.

"Natchoz, California," he said proudly. "Town center."

"Did he say nachos?" Miranda whispered, half giggling, half yawning. "Think we could find some?"

Doubtful. Harper took another look at the "town center." Aside from the gas station, there was a small shack whose sign read only CAFÉ and . . . that was about it. She was used to lame small towns—being born and bred in Grace, CA, lameness capital of the world, it kind of came with the territory. But this wasn't a town, it was a live-in trash heap with its own mailbox.

Leroy filled up their tank, never taking his eyes off Harper's chest. "That'll be forty-seven bucks, ladies," he finally said, hanging up the nozzle. Harper looked at Miranda; taking her cue, Miranda whipped out a credit card. "No can do." Leroy chuckled. "The machine's busted."

"You can't fix it?" Miranda asked anxiously.

Now the chuckle turned into a roar. "Machine's been busted since 1997. You girls got cash?"

Miranda darted her eyes toward Harper and gave her head a quick shake. Translation: They were totally screwed. Harper's wallet, as usual, was empty; she'd been counting on Kane to front her the cash for the Vegas adventure, and Miranda's credit card to get them through the journey.

So now what?

They could make a run for it—hop in the car and drive away before Leroy knew what hit him.

Or—

"You girls ain't got the cash, I'm thinking you could make it up to me another way," Leroy said, giving them a nasty grin. "In trade."

Holy shit.

Beth couldn't stop staring at the bed. She snuck a glance at Reed—he was watching it too.

Her mother thought she was spending the weekend at a friend's house—which showed how little her parents knew of her life these days. She was out of friends. Reed was all she had left. If he disappeared . . .

She refused to let herself think about it. But she still couldn't avoid looking at the bed.

Reed had never pushed her, never pressured her, never expected her to move faster than she was comfortable with or go further than she was ready to go. Not like Adam, who'd pretended he would wait forever—but only waited until a better offer came along. And not like Kane, who never wanted to take no for an answer, and who made Beth feel like a con artist, promising something that she was never intending to deliver.

Why did everything always come down to sex?

Reed was different from other guys in a lot of ways, but Beth wasn't stupid. He was still a guy. And sooner or later, he would surely want to know: When? And then: Why not?

She couldn't avoid it forever. And now, here, the bed filling up half the room, she suspected she couldn't avoid it at all.

"Why don't you guys scope out the casino?" Reed suggested. He shot Beth an easy to interpret look: *Let's ditch these losers, and we can finally be alone.* Part of her couldn't wait—but part of her, as always, was afraid.

"Dude, we have to get ready for tomorrow," Fish pointed out.

"You want to rehearse?" Reed asked incredulously, glancing at the clock. The Blind Monkeys almost never rehearsed—it was one of the reasons they sucked. (Not the only reason, of course: Fish's near total lack of rhythm and Hale's tendency to forget what he was doing in the middle of a song helped too.) "Now?"

"Not rehearse," Fish said, a lopsided grin spreading across his face. *"Prepare."*

Hale got it instantly. They were tuned in to the same wavelength. Or, more accurately, tuned out. "Gotta prepare the *mind*, dude," he said, digging for something in his back-pack. "Get in the zone."

He pulled out the bong. Fish whipped out a lighter and cocked his head at Beth and Reed. "You in?"

"I don't know," Reed hedged. "Maybe we should—"

"We're in," Beth interrupted. She plopped down on the edge of the bed and tugged Reed down next to her. She could tell he wanted to get away from the guys—and probably the bong, too. Ever since they'd started dating, Reed had been cutting back on the pot. Way back.

But no matter: Once she'd discovered that one or two puffs of the miracle drug would crush her doubts, calm her terrors, and clear her head, Beth had been more than happy to pick up his slack. She reached for the bong and, like an old pro, inhaled deeply, savoring the burn.

Along with Reed, this was the only thing that had allowed her to make it through the last couple months. This feeling of lightness and freedom, so different from the suffocating guilt and shame that always threatened to crush her. She needed the escape—and if Reed ever found out why, he would leave her, which made her terror absolute.

Fish reached for the bong, but she held tight and, violating etiquette and caution, inhaled another deep lungful. It would be a long weekend—and she needed all the help she could get.

"Now, *this* is more like it," Harper gushed as they turned onto the Strip. "Civilization. Thank God."

"Mmm-hmmm."

"Okay, how much longer are you going to give me the silent treatment?" Harper asked, exasperated. "I already told you I was sorry. How was I supposed to know that you'd find—"

"Don't say it!" Miranda shrieked. "I'm trying to block it out of my mind forever."

"Okay, okay. How was I supposed to know you'd find that *thing* in the sink. I only volunteered to take the toilet because I thought it would be the grosser job, and it is your birthday weekend, after all."

"Celebrate good times," Miranda deadpanned, and suddenly, in sync, they both burst into laughter. "Did all that really happen?" Miranda sputtered through her giggles. "Or was it just some joint hallucination?"

"I'm not hallucinating the smell," Harper gasped, waving her hands under Miranda's nose. "I washed them ten times back there, and they *still* stink."

Miranda wiggled away, trying to focus on the road. "Don't talk to me about smells," she groaned. "It'll just remind me of—"

"Don't even go there," Harper cautioned her. "You're going to make us both sick."

"Again."

It had turned out that paying for the gas "in trade" had meant helping Larry and his half-toothless wife clean up the "café." It had sustained a fair amount of damage during some kind of brawl earlier that evening: truckers versus motorcyclers, with a few local ranchers thrown in for fun.

Harper and Miranda had been charged with cleaning the bathroom: It wasn't pretty.

Now safely back in civilization, with its lights, non-toxic air, and toilets complete with modern, functional plumbing, they shook with hysterical laughter, and Harper closed her eyes, soaking in the moment. It may have been the most disgusting night of her life, but things between the two of them were actually starting to feel back to normal. There was a time when Harper had feared they would never be close again, mostly because of the things she'd done and said—and all the things she couldn't bring herself to say. *I'm sorry. I need you.* For years, Harper and Miranda had told each other everything. But now Harper was harboring a secret, and Miranda couldn't ever find out the truth. Harper had to stay silent and guarded, always wondering how it was possible that life could go on, day after day, totally normal, that the people around her could smile and laugh like they didn't know the whole thing could come crashing down at any moment, crushing them all.

Harper had to act like nothing was wrong, like she had forgotten what she had done. She had to pretend that she was as confident and carefree as ever, and hide her terror—and her guilt—from everyone. Even Miranda. Especially Miranda, who knew her the best.

How were they supposed to rebuild a friendship with such a massive lie lodged between them? Harper had almost given up hope. But somehow, they'd found their way back to their bickering, bantering norm, and that meant that the long ride, the many detours, and the adventures in raw sewage had all been worth it.

Well, almost.

When they finally found the hotel, they pulled into the lot without registering much of the medieval tackiness of the garish white tower. It was nearly two in the morning, and they could focus on only two things: a hot shower and a soft bed. Both were now, finally, in reach.

They checked in, ignoring all the other Haven High seniors who littered the hallway—it seemed half the school had hit Vegas for the long weekend, and they were all staying at the Camelot, less for its bargain basement prices than for its widely renowned attitude toward its underage denizens: Don't ask, don't tell.

Usually Harper would have lingered amongst the admiring crowd; she never let a moment in the public spotlight go by without putting on a suitable show. But the fewer people who saw—and smelled—her in this state, the better. The girls trekked down a dingy hallway and arrived in front of room 57. Harper swung the door open to discover a small, squalid room with two full-size beds and little else. Miranda immediately dropped down on the one closest to the door, stretching her arms with a satisfied purr. "I could fall asleep right here, right now."

"Perfect, because I call the first shower," Harper said. She dumped her bag and rushed to the bathroom before Miranda could object. She could feel the stink and filth crawling over her skin and needed to scrub it away before she could enjoy the fact that she was finally, after a lifetime of waiting, spending the weekend in Las Vegas.

And after nearly drowning in misery for three months, she planned to enjoy the moment as much as humanly possible.

She opened the door of the bathroom, stepped inside—and screamed.

chapter

2

Adam grabbed a towel and tried to cover himself, but it was too late. Harper had seen everything. Every tan, muscled, gleaming inch of him. She felt faint, and it was all she could do not to lunge across the bathroom and sweep him into her arms, perfect body and all. But she forced herself to stop, and remember: She and Adam were no longer best friends, as they'd been for half their lives. They were no longer in love—*lovers*, she told herself, her mind lingering on the word—as they'd been for too short a time. They were . . . nothing. And she intended to treat him as such.

"What the hell are you doing in our room?" she snapped, trying to regain her equilibrium. *Don't look at his chest,* she told herself. *Don't look at his shoulders. Don't look at his arms. Don't look . . .* This was maybe not the most effective strategy.

"*Your* room?" Adam tugged the towel tighter around himself and took a step forward, as if to escape the bathroom—which would mean his half-naked body brushing right past Harper's, a fact he seemed to realize just in time. He stopped. "This is *our* room. We checked in hours ago!"

"And 'we' would be . . . ?"

"Me. Kane. We. Our room."

And then it all made sense. "Very funny, Geary," she muttered to herself. "Very cute." When Kane had offered to pay for her and Miranda's room for the weekend, Harper had figured it was just an uncharacteristically gallant gesture, an extravagant birthday present for Miranda. (And not that extravagant: According to the website, rooms at the Camelot went for sixty bucks a night.) She should have known better.

"Harper, look," Adam began, "since you're here, maybe we can—"

"I'm out of here," Harper snapped. Why couldn't Adam just give it up? He couldn't get that if he didn't want a relationship with her, she wasn't about to accept his friendship as a consolation prize. Not when she knew what he *really* thought of her. But he just wouldn't take no for an answer, and kept forcing her into these painful state of the union talks. As if she didn't want him in her life, desperately. As if it didn't kill her to remember all the things he'd said when he'd broken her heart, how he hated her, how he could never trust her again, all because she'd made a few not-so-tiny mistakes. And then his belated and halfhearted offer of forgiveness, just because of the accident, just because she'd gotten hurt and Kaia had—

No. She'd resolved not to think about any of that this weekend. She was taking a vacation from her pain and her guilt and everything else that had been weighing her down. Kane *knew* that, and was still pulling this crap? Unacceptable.

But she should have known better than to expect even a brief escape from Adam. Only one thing would make him give up the fight. If he ever found out what she had done to Kaia, Harper knew that would be the end of it. Of everything. And she wasn't ready for that; all the more reason to get away.

She backed out of the bathroom and, without a word of explanation to Miranda, rushed out of the hotel room in search of her target.

"Harper, wait!" Adam called down the hallway. She glanced over her shoulder and, sure enough, he was standing in the hall in only a towel, flagging her down. She didn't stop—but grinned to herself when she realized that he'd let the door slam and lock behind him.

Just before reaching the elevator, she heard a loud thud and a shouted curse.

Apparently he'd realized it too.

Kane sighed and, reluctantly, tore himself away from the stunning blonde to answer his ringing phone. He allowed Harper about thirty seconds of ranting before cutting her off. "I'll meet you in the lobby in five," he promised, snapping the phone shut before she had a chance to respond. He had been expecting her call and, though the face-off could easily be avoided for hours, he preferred to get all potential interruptions out of the way now. The blonde could wait.

This weekend was too important, and his plans too

delicate, to risk interference from a wild card like Harper. And from the sound of it, she was about to get pretty wild.

"What the hell were you thinking?" she raged, as soon as he came into sight.

"Nice to see you, too, Grace," Kane said dryly, spreading out on one of the Camelot's threadbare couches. The pattern had likely once been intended to resemble a medieval tapestry, but now it just looked like Technicolor puke. "Have a good drive?"

"Lovely, thanks for asking." As if the sarcasm had sapped all her energy, she sank into a chair beside him. "Seriously, Kane, what's the deal?"

"The deal with . . . ?"

"Adam? In *my* room? Taking a shower? Any of this ringing a bell?"

Kane smiled innocently. "Adam's up in *our* room— yours, mine, his. Ours. Think of it as one big happy family."

"And it didn't occur to you to mention that this was the plan?"

Kane shrugged. "Did you think I was going to pay for two hotel rooms? I'm not a bank, Grace."

"I—" Her mouth snapped shut, and he knew why. Given that he was footing the bill for the trip, it would be pretty tacky of her to complain about the lodgings. And Harper Grace was never tacky. "I just would have liked some advance notice, that's all," she said sullenly. "You didn't have to ambush me."

"If I'd told you ahead of time, you wouldn't have come," Kane pointed out. Adam and Harper had been feuding for a month now, and Kane was getting sick of it. Not because he felt some goody-two-shoes need to play peacemaker, he told himself. Just because there weren't too many people whose presence he could tolerate; it was troublesome when they refused to share breathing room.

"What do you want me to do?" she asked, a hint of a whine entering her voice. "Make nice and pretend like nothing ever happened between us? Not gonna happen."

"Not my problem, Grace," Kane told her. "Talk to him, don't talk to him, I don't care." Not much, at least. "But this is the only room you've got, so unless you don't plan on sleeping or bathing this weekend—and, no offense, but I think you're already overdue on the latter—you should probably get used to it."

"But—"

"Gotta go," he said quickly, bouncing off the couch. "The most beautiful blonde in all the land is waiting for her knight in shining armor to arrive. I'm hoping to show up first." He wiggled his eyebrows at her, and, miracle of miracles, she cracked a smile. "Now, your mission, and you have no choice but to accept it: Chill out, shower, then grab Miranda and meet me down here in one hour. We're going out."

Harper checked her watch and rolled her eyes. "Geary, it's the middle of the night, and some of us have been on the road for an eternity."

Kane shook his head. "Grace, this is *Vegas.*" Why was he the only person capable of understanding the concept? "Night doesn't exist here. It's a nonstop party, and we're already late."

"I don't know . . ."

"Since when does Harper Grace turn down a party?"

He knew perfectly well since when. That was why he'd

23

insisted she come this weekend and why he'd dragged Adam along for the ride. Harper had been on the sidelines long enough—it was time for her to get back into the game. Whether she wanted to or not.

It was good pot—strong, smooth, decently pure—but not good enough to help Beth sleep through Fish and Hale's impromptu jam session. (Featuring Hale's off-key humming and Fish banging Beth's hairbrush against the wall for a drumbeat.) After an hour of tossing and turning, she finally gave up on trying to sleep—only to discover that Reed was wide awake, lying on his side and staring at her.

"What?" she asked, giggling at the goofy expression on his face.

"Nothing." He gave her a secretive smile, then a kiss. "Let's get out of here."

Still clad in her T-shirt and purple pajama shorts, she crawled out of bed and followed him out the door. They headed downstairs in search of the pool, running into half the Haven High senior class on their way.

Beth didn't care who saw her or how she looked. Only one person's opinion mattered to her these days, and only one person's presence made any difference.

Make that two.

Beth saw her first, and tried to dart down a hallway before they were spotted, but it was too late.

"Well, this is just great," Harper said, lightly smacking her forehead. "As if my weekend weren't perfect enough."

Just ignore her, Beth told herself. She didn't want to get into any more fights with Harper—and not just because she always lost. Yes, Harper had done her best to ruin Beth's life—but Beth's attempt at revenge had nearly succeeded in ruining Harper, permanently. Just as she would always bear the guilt for Kaia's death—*Don't think about that,* she reminded herself—she would always know that Harper could just as easily have been the one who'd died. Harper *was* the one who'd landed in the hospital, gone through painful rehabilitation, emerged pale, withdrawn, and the object of too much curiosity and not a little scorn. They were more than even, although Harper would never—*could never*—know it.

But forgiveness was easier said than done. And even the sight of Harper still made Beth's stomach twist.

"Hey, Harper," she said softly. Reed pressed a hand against her lower back, as if sensing her need for support.

Harper's eyes skimmed over Beth without stopping and zeroed in on Reed. "Having fun with the new girlfriend?" she asked, disdain dripping from her voice. "Guess it's easy for some people to forget."

Harper tried to push past them, but Reed's arm darted out and grabbed her. *Just let it go,* Beth pleaded silently, wanting only for the moment to end quickly, without bloodshed. But she could tell from the look on his face and the tension in his body that he'd already been wounded.

"I haven't forgotten," he told Harper, in a low, dangerous voice. "Kaia would have—"

"Don't say her name," Harper ordered him, her voice tight and her face strained. "Don't say anything. Just *enjoy* yourself. I'm so sure"—though it wouldn't have seemed possible, her tone grew even more sarcastic—"that's what *she* would have wanted."

A moment later, Harper was gone, and Reed was the

one who needed support. But when Beth tried to touch him, he stepped away.

"I'm sorry," she said softly, knowing he wouldn't understand what she was apologizing for.

"It's not you." He wouldn't look at her. "It's nothing."

When they first met, he had talked about Kaia nonstop. But something had changed—Beth never knew what, never wanted to ask. Reed had kissed her and, after that, never spoke of Kaia again. There were moments when his voice drifted off and his eyes stared at something very far away, and she knew, then, that he was wishing for something he couldn't have. But he never said it out loud.

And, though she knew she shouldn't be, Beth was glad. Because the only way she could be with Reed was to force herself to forget. Kaia had died because of her—no, phrasing it that way avoided the truth. She had *killed* Kaia. Accidentally, maybe, but killed nonetheless. And now, reluctantly, guiltily, but undeniably, Beth had taken her place.

She wrapped her fingers around Reed's, half fearing he would pull away. He didn't—but he still wouldn't meet her eyes. "Let's go find the pool," she murmured. He nodded, and she squeezed his hand. He felt so solid, and so safe. He wouldn't disappear, she reassured herself. He would never leave her alone.

Unless he found out the truth.

Then he would be gone forever.

"Down to business," Kane said, rubbing his palms together in anticipation. "How should we kick things off? Blackjack? Poker?"

As Harper and Adam began bickering about where to start—Adam voted blackjack, so Harper, obviously, voted roulette—Miranda lagged behind. She didn't want to admit that she didn't know how to play any of the standard casino games—though she had a vague idea, courtesy of *Ocean's Eleven*, that roulette wouldn't actually require anything other than choosing a color. She'd rented the DVD in anticipation of the big trip, but had been too distracted by George Clooney to glean much more information than that.

She would have been happy enough to spend the whole weekend without coming face-to-face with a dealer, since surely they'd take one look at her height (or lack thereof) and sallow babyface and show her the door. Or whatever it was they did in Vegas when they busted you for a fake ID.

But she didn't want to seem timid or clueless, not in front of Kane—and especially not when he was giving her that anything-goes smile—so she shut up. She was trying to be on her best behavior this weekend. Or rather, her most mature, most carefree, most badass, most Kane-appropriate behavior—especially now that she knew they'd be sharing a room. Okay, so there were two beds and two other people. And Vegas was filled with girls who were much more his type. Maybe it was a statistical impossibility that anything would happen. But Miranda couldn't help letting her imagination have a little fun.

This was, after all, Vegas, where anything could happen . . . which meant that, despite the odds, something *might*.

In the end, they compromised, deciding to start slow, with the slots.

All the action was over at the tables—the slot machines

seemed solely the territory of the blue-haired ladies and a few caved-in old men with bad toupees, waiting for the big payoff. Miranda dug into her pocket and pulled out a fistful of quarters, plugging them into a rain-forest-themed machine that touted itself as the Green Monster. She put her hand on the long, silver lever, then sucked in her breath as a warm, strong grip closed over hers.

"Feeling lucky, beautiful?" Kane murmured from behind her.

Miranda bit down on the corners of her mouth in a pointless attempt to suppress a smile. Was he too thinking about the last time they'd been in a casino together, the last time—the only time—they'd kissed?

Doubtful. For Miranda, it had been the culmination of five years of hoping, dreaming, waiting; for Kane, she knew, it had just been a fast way to liven up a slow afternoon.

Still, he was here, so close that she could feel his chest just grazing her back, and she knew that all she'd have to do was step backward and she would be in his arms.

She stayed where she was, and pulled the lever.

Too late, Miranda thought to wonder: What if she hit the jackpot? If the movies were any guide—and, really, if the movies *weren't* an accurate guide to life, she was totally screwed, since they were pretty much her sole source of information—sirens would blare. Coins would pour out. People would cheer and stare. And the security guards would sweep her away before she could touch a dime.

There was no siren, no jackpot, no cash—and the man who lurched toward her, his breath reeking of gin and his meaty hands grabbing at her chest, was no security guard.

"You're a liar!" he slurred, his hand tightening around Miranda's shoulder as he staggered against her.

"Get the hell off," Kane snapped, shoving himself against the drunk, who squeezed even tighter, nearly pulling Miranda down with him as he stumbled to the floor. For a moment that lasted too long, she was falling, stubby fingers biting into her skin, a leering smile spreading across the man's scarred face. She tugged, she pulled, but his grasp only tightened, and though she tried to scream, her breath caught in her throat, and he was still pulling her down, still grinning, would never let go, and she was powerless, weak—alone.

And then, just in time, Kane ripped her arm free. Miranda shook him off too, and crossed her arms over her chest, squeezing tight and trying to catch her breath. She told herself that nothing had actually happened. No reason to panic, she was fine.

Too out of it to pull himself up, the guy writhed on his back like a crab, pointing at Miranda and howling, *"Liar!"* She couldn't look away. "You're all liars!"

"Can we get a little help here?" Kane called, waving down a swarm of security guards.

Miranda was dimly aware that Harper and Adam had joined her on either side, that Adam's hand was pressing down firmly, protectively on her shoulder—that she was shaking. But none of it really registered.

"It's all going to come out," the drunk moaned, as the guards hauled him off the floor. "No more secrets," he hissed. "Not here." The guards grabbed his arms and began to drag him away, slicing through the crowd of gamblers and disappearing behind the glittering slot machines. A moment later, his howls faded away. There was only giddy laughter, clanging machines, canned jazz, and the occasional hoot of victory. The sounds of Vegas. Like nothing had ever happened.

"You okay?" they all asked Miranda, who nodded like she was.

She forced a smile. "What an asshole, right?"

Crisis averted, Kane's smirk reappeared. "He's right, you know. About Vegas. Everyone here's a liar, but . . ." He narrowed his eyes and pursed his lips in an exaggerated scowl. "It takes a damn good liar to beat Vegas. This is the city of truth."

Adam dropped his hand from Miranda's shoulder and stepped quickly away, and she wondered whether he was thinking the same thing she was. Their secret—one drunken night together, a hookup she barely remembered, a memory they'd both agreed to forget, to bury forever— could ruin everything. And there was no reason for anyone to ever find out—no reason for *Harper* to find out.

Unless Kane was right. Unless there was something here, something in the air, in the oversize drinks or the adrenaline rush, something that forced secrets into the light. . . . Miranda stole a glance at Harper, whose face was ghostly pale, her eyes darting back and forth between Miranda and Adam, her lip trembling.

And Miranda had a horrible thought. She'd worried for weeks that Harper would find out what had happened, would misinterpret an innocent, unimportant, drunken mistake as something more than it was. Something unforgivable.

But what if all that worrying had been a waste—what if Harper already knew?

✧✧✧

All she had wanted was an escape. A return to normalcy.
What an idiot.

Of course Kane was right, Harper thought bleakly. Of
course this was where the secrets came out to play—
everyone drunk all the time, never sleeping, pushing
themselves to the limit, letting their guard down. It was a
disaster waiting to happen.

It was *her* disaster. What if they found out somehow?
The image forced itself back into her head, the one she'd
been trying to forget—the one she'd driven hundreds of
miles to escape. Her hands on the wheel, her foot on the
gas pedal, the world spinning. The flames.

They all pitied her now, which was bad enough. If they
found out she'd been the one behind the wheel, if *Adam*
found out . . .

She told herself she didn't care what he thought, not
anymore. But she knew he could never forgive her for
being a murderer. Why should he? It's not like she had
found a way to forgive herself.

Two days, she thought. *Forty-eight hours.* If she could
survive, stay sane, stay hidden, keep the real her—the
unforgivable her—under wraps for the weekend, it would
be a sign. She had hoped for a vacation from the torment
of her life, but maybe that wasn't what she needed. Maybe
she needed one final test, proof that she could put the past
behind her and focus on normal life, that she could live
with keeping quiet, that she could go on, even here. She
would survive Vegas, and that would be proof—she could
survive anything.

"Forget the drama, guys," Kane said, drawing the group
toward the exit. "We're wasting valuable party time."

"I'm, uh, thinking I might get some sleep," Miranda said, staring at the ground.

"Yeah." Adam's gaze was fixed on the ceiling.

"Maybe they're right, Kane—" Harper began.

"What the hell is this?" He pointed ahead of them to the giant neon sign blinking a few feet away: MIDNIGHT MAGIC BUFFET—24-HOUR FEAST. "It's two-for-one drinks night. What are we waiting for?"

"No more drinking tonight," Adam said. "Not for me."

Kane gaped at the three of them as if they'd sprouted antennae. Then he nodded with sudden understanding. "I get it." He grinned. "I spooked you. Look. I'm sure none of us have any secrets. . . ."

He turned to Harper, who met his stare without flinching. He knew what she had to lose—and she knew he was daring her to chicken out.

"But let's just say, hypothetically, we all do," he continued. "So I suggest a pact. We'll hit the buffet and drink to it. Anything we find out about each other this weekend . . . well, it doesn't count. All secrets forgotten as soon as we leave the city limits. After all, what happens in Vegas—"

"I don't drink to lines that are so old, they have mold growing on them," Harper snapped.

"What happens in Vegas *stays* in Vegas," Kane finished, arching an eyebrow. "Agreed?"

They nodded, and they shook on it. Not that it mattered. Harper knew she was the only one with a secret that really meant something—and there was no way in hell she was risking exposure. Pact or no pact.

"Good. Let's get some cocktails and make it official,"

Kane ordered, charging toward the buffet. "Eat, drink, and be merry, folks, for tomorrow—we do it all over again."

Reed was buzzed.

But it wasn't the drugs. It was her. It was the blond hair, the blue eyes, the cotton-candy lips—all of it like a doll, a picture in a magazine. Picture perfect, but so real, and so unpredictable, starting with her inescapable, unbelievable choice: him. From honor roll to rolling blunts, from superstar to slacker—he didn't even remember how she'd woven her way into his life. She'd just appeared. As if he'd been asleep and then, on waking, there she was. Part of him.

After Kaia . . . Beth had helped him. Not to forget—never, he had promised himself. But Beth had helped him survive the remembering. To live.

He had never asked her why she was hanging around the slums of his life, maybe because he knew it wouldn't last. But Reed had never before cared about the future. Why start now?

"Guess I should have changed into a bathing suit," Beth said, stretching out on the edge of the pool and skimming her bare toes across the water. "We could have gone in the hot tub."

Reed had only ever been in one hot tub in his life, and it was a part of his life that was over now. *It'll be fun,* he heard Kaia's voice say, somewhere in the depths of memory. *Promise.*

"I don't do bathing suits," Reed said, and—except for that one time—it was true. He gestured down to his black AC/DC T-shirt and dark, well-worn jeans, his standard uniform. "This is it."

Beth stood up, her long legs mostly bare beneath the sheer pajama shorts, and joined him on the lounge chair. He scooted over to give her room, but she barely needed any, stretching out alongside him, wrapping an arm over his chest and twining her legs with his. The pool area was nearly empty.

"You can't see the stars here," she mused, resting her cheek against his to look up at the sky. "Too many lights. It's weird."

They'd both grown up under the bright, too-clear desert night sky, where civilization—or what passed for it in Grace—faded away just after nightfall. The city haze was disconcerting, like the sky was closing in on them—or like the stars had disappeared altogether. "Get used to it," he warned her. "Next year . . ."

"Yeah, next year." She fell silent, and in that silence, he saw it all: graduation, summer, and then the day she packed up her stuff and moved to L.A., to college, leaving him to his deadbeat, dead-end life. "About that . . . ," she murmured. "I'm not going."

Reed didn't say anything.

"I'm not—it's not what I want anymore," she said softly, and he could feel her arm tighten around him. She was still searching for the stars. "Maybe if I'd gotten into Berkeley, things would be . . . maybe if a lot of things had happened, or hadn't happened, or—" She stopped, and shivered against him. He began rubbing his hand up and down her arm. "It's not me anymore," she finally said. "It's not what I want."

"So next year, you're just going to . . . ?"

"Stay in Grace. Stay with—" She turned away from the sky, toward him, and rested her hand gently against his cheek. "I know we don't really talk about—I mean, we've never, about next year, but I thought you might . . . be . . . happy."

Happy that she'd given up the only dream she'd ever had, to get the hell out of Grace and move on to something better? Happy that, ever since they'd gotten together, she'd never talked about what she wanted or where she was going, had just lain around on the couch with him listening to his music and smoking his pot? Happy that, unlike him, she had a real future, and she was giving it up?

"Yeah," he said, tipping his head forward and kissing her, still overwhelmed by the taste and feel of her lips, as much as he had been the first time. "I guess I am."

They stuffed themselves on prime rib, shrimp cocktail, fresh fruit in a honey-lime yogurt sauce, jalepeño poppers, garlic-roasted pork loin, fried chicken wings, meat loaf, mashed potatoes, several hearty helpings of chocolate cheesecake and, since none of the half-asleep Midnight Magic staffers seemed to doubt their flimsy IDs, several pitchers of beer.

Merry was an understatement.

"Thish is awesome," Miranda slurred as they stumbled up the Strip back to their hotel. All her ridiculous fears about secrets and lies had long since been forgotten. "I love Vegas."

"Viva Las Vegas!" Harper shouted, flinging her arms in the air. "We love you!"

No one even bothered to stare.

"Shhhh!" Miranda spit out the warning, along with a frothy spray of saliva, and gave Harper a light push—or not

35

so light, as it nearly knocked both of them to the ground.

"Steady," Kane cautioned, pulling her back up. Miranda wanted to say something filled with sparkling wit and sex appeal, but the world was spinning and all she could think to say was, "Woo-hoo! Vegas!"

And then she saw it. Saw him. Twenty feet tall, looming over their heads. Jared Max, lead singer of the Crash Burners, her absolute, all-time favorite band. Jared Max was a rock god—hotter than Adam Levine. Hotter than Justin T. Hotter, even, than Kane.

Miranda sank to her knees in the middle of the sidewalk. "Harper," she gasped. "Harper. Look." She pointed, tipping her head away from the billboard as if it blazed like the face of God.

Crash Burners—LIVE
One Night Only

And a bright yellow band slung across the image, blotting out the drummer's head. SOLD OUT!

"Harper," she moaned. "They're heeeeere. And we're missing it."

Harper joined Miranda on the ground as the guys gaped at them, obviously unable to understand the crisis at hand.

"We're going," Harper said, throwing her arms around Miranda.

"Sold out," Miranda keened, her brain too clogged with fatigue and liquor to form complete sentences, much less rational thought.

"We're going, birthday babe," Harper cried, letting herself fall backward on the sidewalk and squealing as Adam hauled her to her feet. "I promise."

My turn, Miranda thought blissfully, watching Adam prop Harper upright and then turning to stare at Kane, trying to send him a silent message. "Come and get me."

Or had she said that part out loud?

Kane laughed and grabbed her hands, hoisting her up. She didn't want to let go, so instead she let herself sag against him, the Crash Burners and the amazing, inaccessible Jared Max entirely forgotten.

Kane might not have been quite as hot, and he might have been half drunk and all tone deaf, but he was there, he was real and, if only for the too-brief duration of the walk home, he was all hers.

chapter

3

"Ugh, what time is it?" Harper rolled over in the bed and smashed a pillow over her head, trying to block out the painful morning light.

"Shhh, it's still early, go back to sleep," Miranda whispered. She climbed slowly and carefully out of bed—but Harper, half hung over and half drunk, felt every pitch and roll of the bed, as if she were seaborne. She had resolved not to drink much the night before—but the stress in her head and Kane's incessant needling had proven too much. One beer, she'd told herself. One beer, and no more.

She could clearly remember gulping it down and, as the welcome warmth spread through her body, reaching for another. After that, things got a little fuzzy.

Now, too few hours later, even Miranda's careful tiptoes toward the bathroom sounded like elephant footfalls, slamming against the beer-saturated walls of Harper's brain. Forget sleep; it was all she could do to keep her head from exploding.

So she lay awake and very, very still. And she heard everything.

The bathroom door closing.

The water running.

And the unmistakable sound of Miranda puking her guts out.

Harper would know it anywhere.

The toilet flushed and the water kept running—the ever-considerate Miranda would be brushing her teeth now, Harper figured. Gargling mouthwash. And then, right on cue, tiptoeing back to bed.

"You okay?" Harper whispered, rolling toward the edge of the narrow bed to give her friend more room to stretch out.

Miranda smiled ruefully. "Just too much to drink. Sorry for the gross-out factor. Go back to sleep."

But she knew very well that Miranda never threw up when she drank. Harper was self-absorbed, but she wasn't blind. And what she saw was Miranda stuffing her face last night—and unstuffing it in the morning. She didn't do it all the time, not as far as Harper knew, at least. She didn't even do it often—though more often than she had in the fall, before their nightmare year had really begun.

Harper could say something. Miranda always did whatever she said; it formed the basis of their friendship.

But this weekend was supposed to be about making things up to Miranda, celebrating her, not bashing her and her stupid choices. Not driving her away again. Besides, who was she to force Miranda to face reality, when she was doing everything she could to avoid it herself?

Harper took a deep breath and reached out an arm,

fully intending to shake her best friend awake. But then her arm dropped to her side, and, feeling suddenly groggy and overwhelmed, she closed her eyes, hoping for sleep.

This . . . *thing*, this problem that Miranda had, it wasn't an emergency, she told herself. She decided to wait until the time was right.

More to the point: She chickened out.

She chose the same no-risk, no-gain approach she took to all her problems these days: ignored it, and hoped it would go away.

Beth was nearly asleep on her feet. They'd crawled out of bed at 7 a.m., hoping to beat the inevitable crowds at the All-American Band Battle registration area. But that was wishful thinking. Judging from the way they looked—and smelled—some of these bands must have camped out in the auditorium all night; Beth and the Blind Monkeys were at least fifty people back in line, which so far had translated into a painful hour of scoping out the competition.

When they finally made it to the small metal folding table at the head of the room, a sullen girl with thick purple eyeliner and matching purple dreads handed Beth a stack of forms without looking up. "Band name?" she asked, sounding almost too bored to bother taking another breath.

Beth looked around at the guys, waiting for one of them to speak, but none of them did. Apparently, she was now groupie, roadie, and form-filler-outer. So much the better. The more responsibilities she had, the more they would need her. "Blind Monkeys," she said, half proud to be a part of something and half embarrassed by the knowledge that, in fact, she wasn't.

The girl scanned her clipboard, then sighed in irritation. "Not on here. Did you send in your preregistration forms?"

"Of course—" Beth started to say. Then she caught the glance exchanged between Fish and Hale. "Guys?"

Fish twirled a strand of his long, blond hair; Hale just stared at her blankly. "Did you mail it in?" She'd filled out the forms, signed their names, bought the stamps, put it all together—all they'd had to do was take it to the post office to send it off. She and Reed would have done it themselves, but the guys had volunteered.

"We may have . . ." Fish scuffed his toe against the shiny hardwood floor. "There was this girl . . ."

"And the pizza, dude, don't forget the pizza," Hale added, his face lighting up at the memory.

"Yeah, and then this guy, and we had to get the truck for him—"

"And the girl was hot, man," Hale explained, punching Reed's shoulder. "Smoking hot, you know?"

Reed ran a hand across his face, mashing it against his eyes. "You didn't send it in," he said, without looking. It wasn't a question. "Let's go. We're screwed."

At the sound of Reed's hoarse, gravelly voice, the girl at the table finally looked up. Her eyes widened, and her surly expression morphed into a half smile. "Not so fast, boys," she told them, fingering the black, studded collar that hugged her neck. "You come a long way for this?"

"We were on the road all day yesterday," Beth said. The girl didn't appear to notice. She was too busy staring at Reed. And he'd noticed.

"Can't believe the shitty van made it the whole way,"

he told her, flashing a rare smile. "We're probably stuck here for good."

The girl leaned forward, giving all of them a good glimpse of the dark crease at the base of her neckline. (Could it still be called a neckline when it dipped nearly to her navel?) "That wouldn't be the worst thing in the world," she said.

"Maybe not," Reed agreed, reaching back and rustling the back of his head, which made his wild black hair fly out in all directions. Beth couldn't help admire the way his sinewy biceps moved between his tight, black T-shirt—and she wasn't the only one.

She's flirting with him, Beth thought in disgust. And, what was worse—*he's flirting back.*

"I'm Starla," the girl said, extending a hand to Reed. When he took it, she didn't shake, just gripped his hand firmly, holding it in midair for a too-long moment. "That's Starla with a star." She turned his hand over and, grabbing a ballpoint pen, illustrated on his palm:

STAR*LA

Beth felt like she was going to be sick.

"Reed," he told her, without snatching his hand back.

"And I'm Beth," Beth said, stepping closer to her boyfriend. She wanted to wrap an arm around his shoulder, the universal sign for *He's mine and you can't have him,* but she was afraid of looking petty. And what if he stepped away?

"I might be able to slip you guys into the schedule," Star*la said.

"You won't get in trouble?" Reed asked.

How sweet, Beth thought sourly. *He's looking out for her.*

She wasn't usually the jealous type—but then, until recently, she hadn't been the Reed type either. Things change.

"I'm sure it'd be worth it," the girl assured him. "After all, you could be 'America's Next Superstars,'" she said with mock enthusiasm, mouthing the contest slogan.

"Never gonna happen," Reed promised her, though he leaned over the table and began filling out the forms she'd handed him.

"Have a little hope, Reed Sawyer," Star*la said brightly, reading the name upside down off one of the forms. She pulled out a handful of buttons, each bearing the label #32. Two went to Beth, who handed them off to Fish and Hale. Star*la took the third one and pinned it onto Reed's shirt, just below his breastbone. Beth noticed that her fingernails were painted black and a small, thorny rose was tattooed along the length of her inner wrist. She caught Reed noticing it too. "This is Vegas." Star*la slapped her hand flat against his chest. "Anything can happen."

"How can you watch that shit?" Kane flicked his hand toward the TV, where a bright blue squirrel was chasing a talking bird through the magic forest.

"The question is, how can you *not* watch it?" Harper asked, stretching her legs to the ceiling, then flopping them back down to the bed with a satisfied sigh. "It's Saturday morning. These are Saturday morning cartoons. Had you no childhood? Have you no soul?"

Kane shrugged. When he was a kid, he'd spent Saturday morning helping his brother clear up the remains of last night's partying before their father came home. As for the dubious existence of his soul . . . it wasn't a question for a hungover Saturday morning in Sin City.

"I've got a phone call to make," he told the girls. "If this slacker wakes up"—he gestured at Adam, still conked out in his sleeping bag—"tell him not to touch my aftershave."

"Yeah, we'll make sure he knows your makeup and hair gel is off-limits too, Tyra," Harper mocked. He tossed a pillow at her, hitting Miranda, instead. She grabbed it with a giggle and threw it back at him, the worn gray tank top she'd slept in rising up to reveal a taut band of skin above her low-riding boxers.

"Back in a flash, ladies. Try not to miss me too much." He tipped an imaginary hat to them and slipped out to the hallway. Let his friends sleep in and waste the day away watching TV. Kane had been up for an hour or two and was already showered, impeccably dressed, and ready to go. He just had a few details to finalize.

He dialed the number. "I'm here," he said into the phone, before his contact had a chance to speak. "When can we meet?"

"Do you have the cash?"

"Do you have the stuff?"

There was a pause. "I have what I said I would. You shouldn't have to ask."

Kane always had to ask. "Just tell me where." A few girls he vaguely recognized from Haven High wandered down the hall in their pajamas, giggling and blushing when they spotted him. He waved, flashed the famous smirk, then, as soon as they passed, turned toward the wall and hunched over the phone. Normally he loved nothing more than to see and, more importantly, be seen; but this was nobody's business but his own. "Where and when?"

"Two thirty. At the Fantasia, by the fountain in the rear lobby. You know the place?"

"I'll find it," Kane said, and snapped the phone shut. He checked his watch: He had almost two hours to kill. Two hours in paradise—not usually the kind of thing he minded. But he was impatient to get the meeting over with, the deal done. He headed back into the room to swig some mouthwash and grab his wallet, his mind already running through all his options for pleasure in the pleasure center of the world.

He never needed a reason to go to Vegas, his haven away from Haven. It had everything he could ever want: booze, blues, girls, gambling, endless possibilities. But a little added incentive never hurt anyone, and as far as he was concerned, there was no better incentive than cold, hard cash.

As much of it as possible.

"What do you mean you're leaving?" Harper pressed herself against the bathroom door, blocking his exit. It was far too early in the morning for her plans to be falling so completely apart.

Kane hoisted himself up onto the bathroom sink and swung his feet off the edge. "I mean, I'm walking out the door, closing it behind me, walking down the hall, getting on the elevator—"

"Shut up," Harper snapped. "It's too early for sarcasm."

"It's past noon," Kane pointed out.

"Whatever. Are you forgetting what we talked about last night?"

Kane tipped his head to the side, tapped his chin, and pretended to think. "World peace?"

He could be such a bastard sometimes—and yet so useful. At least when he decided to play nice. "We talked about the concert tomorrow. The Crash Burners, remember?" His face remained an impenetrable blank. "You promised to help me track down some tickets today. For Miranda?"

Kane shook his head. "Any promises made under the influence are null and void. Look it up in the rulebook."

"Geary, you're *always* under the influence of something or other," Harper pointed out.

He rewarded her with a smile. "And now you understand why I never keep a promise."

"You're pathetic." So much for Miranda's fabulous birthday weekend. So much for *her* promise, drunken or not. What was she supposed to do all day instead: lie around the room feeling sorry for herself?

"And you love it." Kane hopped off the sink and scooped Harper out of the doorway. "Look, I can give you the name of a guy I know, he works the controls at the Oasis Volcano, he'll probably be able to help. Go see him—and bring Adam."

Harper wrinkled her nose. "Why would I do that?" The less time spent with Adam this weekend, the better. It was hard enough shutting him out of her life when he wasn't around. But when he was right in front of her, staring at her with those "love me" puppy-dog eyes, how was she supposed to keep her emotional distance? She was already this close to letting him back in—it was only running into Beth last night that had snapped her back to reality, reminding her that she'd never be able to match up to the pretty princess in Adam's eyes. And she was sick of spending all her energy to claw her way into second place.

"This guy . . . he's got some issues. He won't talk to strangers—he'll only help you if he thinks he's dealing with me. And unless you want to dress in drag . . ."

Harper rolled her eyes. "I suppose Adam's got a Kane mask stashed away in his suitcase somewhere?"

"I've never met the guy face-to-face," Kane explained. "He does me favors sometimes, when he's in the mood. Just get Adam to say he's me. It'll be almost as good as having the real thing."

"You know what would be even better?" Harper drawled. "*Having* the real thing. You're really going to ditch me and leave me with . . . *him*?"

Kane gave her a condescending pat on the head. "It's for your own good, Grace. So take it or leave it."

She hated to lose. And only Kane knew quite how much—which was why, she was sure, he took such a special pleasure in beating her. "I'll take it." She sighed, then decided to press her luck. "And I'll take something else, too." She opened her palm and held it out in front of him.

"You want me to give you five?" he asked, willfully obtuse. He slapped her palm lightly. "If you insist."

"More than five, Geary. If you're going to send me off on some wild-goose chase looking for your skeezy errand boy, I'm going to need to find a way to keep Miranda occupied. And that's going to cost."

Kane grabbed her hand and, firmly, pushed it back down to her side. "Just take her with you."

"It's got to be a surprise," Harper insisted. "I don't want her to suspect anything."

"And you don't think dragging me into the bathroom and locking the two of us in isn't going to make her just a little suspicious?" Kane asked, raising an eyebrow.

She hated that he could do that. In junior high, she'd spent hours in front of the mirror trying to train her eyebrow muscles to work independently of each other, but she'd failed miserably. Maybe the skill was genetic—if so, Harper guessed, it was probably linked to the genes for selfishness, smugness, asshole-ishness, and all the other qualities Kane Geary carried so proudly.

She couldn't help but admire him.

But that didn't mean she was going to back down.

"Let me worry about that," she told him. "Just help me out with this. If you don't care about helping me, think of Miranda." From the look on his face, Harper knew it was the right card to play. She knew that, no matter how much Miranda might wish for it, there was no way in hell Kane would ever fulfill her sad little romantic fantasy and declare his love. But Kane knew it too, and Harper suspected that somewhere beneath his preening, posing shell, he felt a little sorry.

Apparently not sorry enough. "Nice try. No sale."

Harper shrugged. "Okay."

"Okay?" He peered at her suspiciously.

"Sure." She gave him a perky grin. "No problem. Don't worry about it."

"What's the catch?"

Ah, he knew her so well. "No catch. No hard feelings. I'm sure the three of us will have a lovely day together."

"The three of you?"

"The three of *us*," Harper corrected him. "Miranda, me, and *you*—together. Just like the Three Musketeers. The Supremes. The Three Tenors. You get the idea. One happy threesome—"

Kane's smile twitched, and broadened.

"Not like that, gutter-brain," she snapped. "Like this. You head out on your mysterious mission, we follow. Wherever you go, we go. Whatever you do, we do. And whatever it is you're up to this afternoon, we—"

"Spare me the tedious details, I get it. You win."

She met his bitterness with a beatific smile. "Music to my ears."

"Just take the cash and let me out of here." He pulled out his wallet and handed her a credit card. "Send her to a spa for the afternoon. Girls love that shit, right? Massages, scented candles, mani-pedis, whatever."

Harper bit back the urge to point out that, between the two of them, Kane seemed the far more likely candidate for spa-hopping. From his Theory shirt to his Diesel jeans, he was Grace's only known metrosexual, and damn proud of it. But, credit card not yet in hand, she decided silence might well be the best policy.

He handed her the credit card, along with a scrap of paper bearing the name and number of his "guy," and then, with a final infuriating elevation of his left eyebrow, reached for the doorknob.

"So where *are* you going in such a hurry?" she asked, knowing better but too hung over for caution.

"I'll tell you later," he promised.

Well, that was unexpected.

"Really?"

"No."

The awkwardness was new—but it was getting old.

Last night had been their first uninterrupted stretch of time together in weeks, and Harper's frosty demeanor had given way after the first pitcher of beer. Things had been almost easy between them, and Adam had allowed himself to hope. Until this morning, when she'd once again frozen him out.

Adam knew Harper well enough to understand his odds: hopeless. If he wouldn't give her what she wanted—and he couldn't—she wouldn't give him the satisfaction of revealing how much she needed him. And maybe, these days, it wasn't much at all.

So, after a few frosty unpleasantries, Adam had gone back to bed. But not to sleep. How was he supposed to sleep, knowing she was sitting only a few feet away from him, maybe waiting for him to say something—or, for all he knew, waiting for him to blink out of existence once and for all.

He didn't even know why she was still there. He had expected her to leave along with Kane and Miranda, but instead, she'd stayed in bed, stretched out with her feet kicking the pillows, staring at the television. *Say something,* he told himself. *Sit up, start a conversation.*

But he didn't know how. Even in the beginning, when they'd first become friends, they had always understood each other. Always known what the other was thinking. It had been effortless. Now, blundering around in the dark, he didn't even know where to start hunting for the light switch.

There had been that brief period of weirdness in fifth grade, when Harper woke up and realized Adam was a boy, and Adam—courtesy of a windy day, a gauzy skirt, and a bout of humiliated tears—clued in to the fact that even tomboys had their girly moments. Harper stopped wrestling him to the ground and demanding the remote control. Adam stopped mixing her dolls with his action figures. Harper stopped using her Fisher-Price telescope to peer in his bedroom window, and Adam started dating a pretty blond sixth grader named Emma Farren, who once poured red paint all over Harper's spelling homework.

It was a long week.

Long and lonely—and before too long, Adam and Harper mutually decided to ignore the sticky boy-girl thing and proceed as if nothing had changed. Which, other than Harper's perfect curves and Adam's elephant-size libido, it hadn't.

Since then, he had always been able to count on her, and she on him. They'd climbed the social ladder together, Adam with the unconscious ease of a blond jock built for adoration, Harper with ruthlessness and a fierce determination. Adam had grown cavalier—with his grades, his games, his girls—and Harper had grown vicious, but they'd stayed loyal to each other. Without question, without doubt, without exception.

And then, in short order, it had all been destroyed.

Adam had fallen in love with Beth; a jealous Harper had torn the two of them apart. Adam, oblivious, had fallen in love all over again, with Harper—or with the Harper he thought he knew. And when the truth came to light, when he realized who Harper had become and what she was capable of, he'd pushed her away.

How was he supposed to know that days later, she would be lying in a hospital bed, pale and unconscious, as he waited and wondered and wished he could take back every word? And what was he supposed to do when she woke up and mistook his concern for forgiveness, when she rejected his offer of friendship because he refused to deliver anything more?

She wanted her boyfriend back; he wanted his best friend back. She couldn't forget how happy they'd been; he couldn't forget what she'd done, how she'd lied. Adam just wanted to go back to the beginning, before things got ugly and cruel—but Harper preferred to go forward, alone.

And now here they were, awkward and miserable. At least, he was miserable. It had been a mistake to let Kane talk him into this trip, into this ridiculous ambush, as if the element of surprise would shake Harper's resolve. He needed to get out of here and forget about the whole thing for a while. He decided he would get up, slip into some clothes and out of the room, so quietly and quickly that she wouldn't have time to react—or, at least, he wouldn't have time to dwell on how she chose not to.

Then, without warning, she spoke.

"I need your help," she said, and he could guess how much effort it cost her to keep her voice casual and even as she uttered her four least favorite words.

He couldn't make a big deal about it. She was on the

line, nibbling at the bait—he had to reel her in slowly, before she got spooked.

"Mmmph." He sat up, realizing she must have known all along that he wasn't asleep.

"I got Miranda the full treatment," she said, sounding almost as if she were talking to herself, "which should give us about six hours. But we have to start now."

Maybe he should have resented the fact that she just assumed he would go along with her—but he knew what it meant. She knew she could still count on him when she needed him.

And she needed him now.

Adam suppressed the urge to jump out of bed and embrace her—or, better yet, shake her and force her to admit that her whole act was a sham, and she needed their friendship as much as he did.

Slow and steady, he cautioned himself. *Patience.*

"I was going to watch the game," he complained, grabbing the remote and switching to ESPN.

Harper switched off the TV. "Look, I don't want to spend the day with you any more than you want to spend it with me, but I'm stuck, and I . . ."

"Yeah?"

She propped her hands on her hips and stared down at him impatiently. "Are you going to make me say it again?"

"You . . ."

Harper rolled her eyes.

"You need . . ."

Harper still stayed silent, though Adam was sure he saw the ghost of a smile playing at the edge of her lips.

"You . . . need . . . my . . . help," he concluded triumphantly.

She sighed. "What you said."

"Well, since you put it so sweetly . . ." Adam climbed out of bed. "I'm all yours."

"Lucky me," she muttered, shutting herself up in the bathroom so she wouldn't have to watch him change.

"Lucky us," Adam said quietly, to himself. She'd opened a door—to possibility, to reconciliation, to the past. No matter what, he wouldn't let it slam shut again.

chapter

4

"I just don't get it," Miranda said again. "What am I supposed to *do* at a spa?"

Kane shook his head. It was almost charming, her complete lack of comprehension about one of the most fundamental feminine pleasures. He spent most of his life on the arm of beautiful girls who were more primped and pampered than a Westminster Dog Show poodle. Miranda's awkward naïveté was almost charming. "Not my area of expertise," he reminded her—while making a mental note that, speaking of pampering, his nails were looking a little too ragged these days. "I've just been informed that I'm to drop you off at the spa and make sure you go inside. My mission ends there."

"Door to door service? Ooh-la-la."

"Only the best for the birthday girl," he said, leading her to the entrance of Heavenly Helpers. He grabbed her hand and, in his standard farewell gesture—at least when it came to pretty girls—turned it palm down, lifted it, and brushed it with his lips. Most girls giggled at the faux chivalry, but Miranda, despite a faint reddish tinge to her cheeks, didn't crack a smile.

"You're too kind, sir," she said mockingly. And, with a quick flip of the wrist, she brought his hand to her lips and mirrored his gesture.

"And they say chivalry's dead," he joked.

"They say feminism's dead too," she shot back, "but here you are, working nonstop on our behalf."

"I do what I can," he said modestly.

"Kane Geary," she said, presenting him to the non-existent audience with a Vanna White flourish, "helping women one bimbo at a time."

"You wound me, Stevens," he said, clasping his hands to his heart.

"Every chance I get," she agreed. And now, finally, he got a smile.

She wasn't hot, he reflected. Pretty, maybe, in an understated way, if you liked them short, pale, and skinny. Definitely not his type, though he was certain—despite her blustering and her refusal to stage a sequel to their last hookup—she wished she were. But she was a much better kisser than he'd expected, and there were times during these conversational jousts, when her face got flushed, her voice high, and her eyes bright, when he wished he could just drop the game and grab her and—

Whoa. He stopped himself abruptly. That was not a place his mind was supposed to go with Miranda Stevens. Good kisser or not. This was Vegas, land of gold fringe and stiletto heels; he refused to allow Miranda, with her ill-fitting jeans, faded T-shirts, and assorted neuroses, into his fantasies, much less his schedule.

"Door-to-door service, and here's the door," he said, losing the flirtatious tone. "Have fun."

Miranda raised her eyebrows. "Sure you don't want to see for yourself what—"

"Another time," he cut in, before he could get sucked into another round of volleying. He waved and backed away before she could say anything more, and didn't turn around to check that she'd stepped inside the spa, Harper's instructions be damned.

It didn't stop him from being sorry to see her go.

Shake it off, he warned himself. *You've got business.*

It was a five-minute drive to the Fantasia—or would have been, had traffic on the Strip not been at a standstill. Kane had never considered himself a small-town guy, even though he'd spent his life in a place where the prairie dog population outnumbered the human one. But he couldn't help gaping at the flashing lights, packed sidewalks, and feverish motion of everyone and everything in sight.

Someday, he vowed, he would live in a place like this; someday, he would run it.

He dropped off the car with the valet and made his way to the back lobby, trying to ignore the many temptations along the way. (Out of the corner of his eye, he caught a glimpse of a redhead with a glass of whiskey in one hand and a deck of cards in the other: one-stop shopping for all his vices.) His contact was already waiting.

"Maryjane420@xmail.com, I presume?" A tall, wispy guy in his early twenties stepped out from behind a column, extending a hand.

Kane noted the guy's woven hemp necklace and scraggly blond goatee—he was a dead ringer for the dealer who'd hooked them up. Not a huge surprise; these Berkeley guys liked to play at being nonconformists, but with the tie-dye and the Birkenstocks, they might as well be wearing a uniform. "Kane," he said, giving the guy a firm handshake. He couldn't afford his customary caustic snark; another temptation to avoid for the sake of business.

"Jackson," the guy replied, flashing a peace sign.

Kane suppressed a snort. If this loser was as happy-go-lucky as he looked, things would go very smoothly indeed.

"So are you the small-talk type, or are you ready to see the merchandise?" Jackson dropped his faded gray backpack to the ground and began to unzip it without waiting for an answer.

"Here?" Kane hissed. His contact had assured him this Jackson guy was 100 percent professional, a safe way to kick his own business up to the next level. But was he too dim to realize that Las Vegas was closed-circuit-TV central? That was the problem with Nor Cal dealers, Kane had found— too much sampling of their own merchandise had fried their brains. Kane, on the other hand, prided himself on restraint. He was only too happy to supply others with whatever they needed, as a gesture of goodwill—and good profit—but he wasn't about to follow them down the rabbit hole.

"Here, there, anywhere," Jackson babbled. "That's the beauty of it." And before Kane could stop him, he pulled something out of his bag. It was about four inches long and wrapped in orange and brown foil.

It was perfect.

"'Munchy Way,'" Kane read off the wrapper, admiring

the logo's similarity to the familiar Milky Way swirl. This was even better than he'd hoped.

"And here's a couple Pot-Tarts," Jackson said, pressing a small stack of foil squares into his hand. "For later." He grinned proudly. "Cool, yeah?"

They looked almost real. It was the perfect product for Kane, who was tired of serving as a go-between for his brother's skeevy dealer buddies and their junior high customers. With a gimmick like this, he could attract a bigger crowd, a *better* crowd—and the operation would be all his. He'd pocket all the money, carry all the risk; and, with no one else involved, he could be sure that the risks were kept to an absolute minimum.

Kane didn't trust anyone but himself—but he trusted himself absolutely.

He ripped open the foil and took a bite. It was the familiar gooey chocolate goodness—with an equally familiar, almost bitter undertaste.

"I've got Rasta Reese's, Buddafingers, Puff-a-Mint Patties, whatever you need," Jackson told him, zipping the bag shut.

"This could work," Kane mused, hoping to disguise his enthusiasm. Jackson might have been a dippy hippie, but he was also a pro; this was, on the other hand, Kane's first big buy, and he wanted to do it right. "What's your price?"

"Not so fast," Jackson said, and the foggy expression vanished, replaced by a look that was sharp, canny, and hungry. "I don't know you, I don't know if I can trust you. I definitely don't need you. So why don't you start by telling me what *you* can do for *me*."

The rapid shift caught Kane off guard, but not for long. "Meaning?"

"Meaning, if you want in, I'm going to need some insurance—and I'm going to need some incentive."

It turned out that the Oasis Volcano was really a giant fountain with reddish water cascading down its sides and spurts of fire shooting out of the top. Like everything else in Vegas, Harper was discovering, the plastic mountain was impressive until you got up close—then it was just tacky and sad.

"One thing I forgot to tell you," Harper said as they approached the operator's booth in search of Kane's "guy." She hadn't forgotten—she'd just been trying to keep conversation to a minimum until absolutely necessary. "You're Kane."

Adam wrinkled his forehead. "Try again. I'm *Adam*."

She used to think it was so cute when he tried to be funny—even when he failed. Especially when he failed.

"This guy will only talk to Kane, but they've never met face-to-face," she explained impatiently. "Kane called and told him we were coming—I mean, that he was coming. You know what I mean. So you're just going to have to play the part."

"I'm going to have to play the part . . . ," he prompted, his eyes twinkling.

She sighed. Magic word time. "Please."

The operator's booth was stationed in the back of the volcano, behind a low fence that Adam vaulted easily. He reached out his arms for Harper. "Want help?"

"I got it, thanks," she said brusquely, and scrabbled over,

catching the edge of her shirt in one of the barbs. She didn't notice until she slid down to the other side and her shirt, still caught at the top of the fence, flew up over her head. Harper slammed her arms over her chest, trying to tug the shirt down with one hand and extricate herself with the other, a move that would have been possible only if she'd picked up some triple-jointed tricks from the local Cirque du Soleil troupe.

"Still got it?" Adam asked, standing a couple feet away with his arms folded.

"I'm just—almost—" After nearly stretching her arm out of its socket, Harper gave in to the inevitable. "Get me off this thing, will you?" And a frustrated moment later, "Please?"

Adam stood in front of her and, reaching an arm around either side, fumbled with the back of her shirt. It seemed to take a very long time, and Harper spent it trying not to notice that his head was so close to hers that she could smell his shampoo. She didn't want to meet his eyes—or worse, let her gaze travel down his body, lingering on her favorite parts—but she refused to look away.

"You're free," he told her. But she was still locked into place by his arms on either side.

She ducked underneath and escaped. "Let's do this."

"I'm Kane?" he asked, as she knocked on the window of the tiny booth.

"You're Kane," she confirmed, crossing her fingers. Adam's idea of acting usually involved bad foreign accents and funny hats. This could end poorly.

The door swung open, and a bulky guy with acne and a shaved head beckoned them inside. "Yo, Jenkins, dude, how's it hanging?" Adam asked, giving the guy one of those handshake/slap/snap things wannabe skater dudes exchange on MTV.

Harper tried not to roll her eyes. This could end *very* poorly.

"I'm Carl," the guy said, extending a hand to Harper. "Carl Jenkins. Kane's told me how much he likes beautiful women, but . . . wow."

Harper knew she was supposed to be flattered, not grossed out. Fortunately, she was a better actor than Adam. Practice makes perfect, right?

"That's so sweet, Carl," she said, giving his hand a gentle squeeze before dropping it (and resisting the urge to wipe the grease off on her jeans).

"You mackin' on my lady?" Adam asked, wrapping an arm around Harper's waist. Without warning, he began to tickle her side—she squealed and sprung away. "You know you want me, Mandy," he said, grabbing her hand and pulling her back against him. "I mean, uh, Sandy. I mean . . ." Adam gave Carl an exaggerated wink, and then shrugged. "Who can keep track? All I know is, she sure does come in handy!"

"I can imagine," Carl said, with a low whistle. "You're like my hero, man."

"That's why they call me LL-Cool K," Adam joked. "Ladies *Love* Cool Kane."

Oh. My. God. Harper buried her face in Adam's shoulder as the giggles burst out of her, hoping Carl would mistake it for a sudden burst of affection for her man. She only wished Kane could be here to see exactly what Adam thought of him.

And imagining that, she began to laugh even harder.

Adam patted her heaving shoulders. "Her pet cat died this morning," he explained. "Her name was Lady. So every time she hears the word, well . . ." He dropped his voice to a loud whisper. "You know girls."

After a moment, Harper regained control of herself and looked up, her face stained with laughter-induced tears. Perfect. "I'll miss her a lot," she said, her breath still ragged and torn by the occasional leftover giggle. "But at least I've got Kane here to comfort me." She patted him back. Hard.

"But there's only one thing that would *really* comfort her, Jenkins, you know what I mean?" Adam winked.

"Oh . . . uh . . . I'd give you some privacy, but I can't leave the booth—but there's this storage room in the lobby where no one goes and—"

"Ew—no!" Harper shivered. She didn't want any part of Carl's gross fantasies. "I mean, that's not what he meant. Tell him, *Kane.*"

"Tickets," Adam said, and now he was the one choking back laughter. Harper could feel his body tremble. "For the Crash Burners tomorrow night—they're her favorite. And when we talked on the phone, you said . . . ?"

"Oh, yeah." Carl rubbed the back of his neck. "Look man, I know I owe you, for that other thing you did."

"Yeah, uh, that thing. That was rough," Adam said quickly. "You definitely owe me, Jenkins."

"And I thought I could deliver, but turns out these tickets are impossible to get."

"There's nothing you can do?" Harper asked, dropping the damsel-in-distress act. "There's got to be *something.*"

"There's one person who might be able to help you,"

Carl said, giving Harper a shy smile. He tore out a page from his magazine—*Guns and Ammo*, Harper noted with displeasure—and scrawled down a name and address on the back. "She works at the Stratosphere, up top, on the coaster. Tell her I sent you, and maybe you'll get what you're looking for."

Adam made another attempt at the lame handshake combo. "Thanks, dude. I'll remember this."

"So next time I need, you know . . . you'll . . . you know?"

"Oh, totally." Adam gave him a mock salute. "You're my guy."

"Awesome."

"Yeah, yeah, totally awesome," Harper added, impatient to get going. "Great to meet you and all, but we've got to . . ."

"Yeah." Carl checked his watch. "Holy shit, it's time for the eruption. I've gotta kick you guys out. But stick around, you'll love it."

Adam escorted Harper out, and, since the fence unlocked from the inside, they made it back to the tourist zone unscathed.

"What was *that*?" Harper asked, bursting into laughter once they were a safe distance away.

"What?"

"*That!* You were supposed to be acting like Kane, not like . . . like some *Saturday Night Live* lounge lizard."

"He bought it, didn't he?" Adam asked indignantly.

"Ladies *love* cool Kane." Harper shook with laughter, and soon Adam joined in. "Seriously? LL-Cool K? I mean, *seriously?*"

Adam shrugged and gave a gee-whiz smile. "What can I say? The ladies love me."

Something about the line stopped her cold, and her smile faded away. "We should get going," she said, already feeling the distance beginning to grow between them. "We don't have all day."

"Wait." He reached for her arm, but pulled back just as his fingers grazed her skin. "Wait," he said again. "Let's at least stay for the show."

As he spoke, a loud rumbling began, deep inside the volcano, which looked even faker now that Harper had seen the switches, dials, and the guy who made it run. But it couldn't hurt to stay for just a few minutes and see what the big deal was.

They inched closer to the front of the crowd, stealing a spot on the guardrail at the edge of the fountain pool, and waited. Soon the volcano began bubbling and burbling, and then a huge plume of flame burst out of the top, followed by a geyser of red water, arcing out of the crater mouth and out toward the crowd.

Harper leaped back. Adam, too slow on the uptake, merely stared slack-jawed at the sky as a wall of bloodred water crashed down on him.

Another burst of flame, a puff of smoke, and the eruption had ended. Adam rubbed the water out of his eyes and began wringing out his sopping T-shirt. "That was . . ." He looked down at himself, soaked to the skin. ". . . unexpected."

Harper felt another surge of giggles rippling through her. It felt good to laugh again. "I don't know why you didn't see it coming," she sputtered. "You said it yourself, LL-Cool Kane. Lava Loves Cool Kane!"

"Very funny," Adam growled. "You know what's even

funnier?" He lunged toward her and gave himself a mighty shake. Water flew everywhere.

"Watch it!" she cried, twisting away.

"I think you mean, watch *out*." He chuckled, and lunged toward her again, wrapping his arms around her and pressing her against his soaking body. She struggled playfully for a moment, but these were arms that regularly shot fifty free throws a day. They didn't give. "Thanks for helping me dry off," he teased, rubbing his wet arms up and down her back.

"Thanks for ruining my outfit," she complained, but she stopped struggling. He didn't understand how hard it was for her, having him so near, touching her, *holding* her, and knowing that he didn't mean it, didn't want her.

Knowing that he didn't think she was worthy of him— and that he was right.

The moment she let down her guard and let him in, just a little, waves of pain came along for the ride.

Let go of me, she thought, but couldn't force herself to say, even though it would be for her own good.

Adam held on tight.

Reed slammed his hand down on the guitar strings in disgust. "Fish, you're still coming in a beat too late after the bridge!"

Fish snorted and pointed at Hale. "If this dude would actually follow my cues, I wouldn't have to—"

"If you picked up the tempo and—"

"At least I'm not playing in the wrong key," Fish shot back.

"At least I'm *playing*—a monkey could bang sticks together. What I do takes talent," Hale argued.

"You're right," Fish agreed, slamming his stick against the cymbal. "Too bad you don't have any."

Bah-dum-bum. Beth shifted in the folding chair, searching for some position that wouldn't leave the metal bar digging into her lower back. Star*la had squeezed them into a rehearsal room in the basement of the Fantasia for some last-minute fine-tuning—but so far, the band had barely managed to make it through a single song.

"Maybe you guys should take a break?" Beth suggested.

Fish and Hale exchanged a glance. "Dude, can you tell your girlfriend to chill?" Fish said quietly to Reed—but not quietly enough.

"She's kind of freaking me out, just staring at us like that," Hale added.

"She's right here, guys," Beth said loudly. "She can hear everything you say."

"Dude, it's just that—"

"Forget it." Beth stood up, realizing that her left foot had fallen asleep. She stamped it against the ground, trying to get rid of the pins and needles. "I'm going to take a walk."

Reed hurried over to her and tipped his head against hers so that their foreheads met. "You don't have to go," he said softly. "They're just . . . we kinda suck right now, and—"

She ran her hand lightly up the back of his neck, playing with some loose strands of curly hair. "You guys are great," she assured him. "You just need practice. And you don't need me throwing things off."

Reed kissed her on the cheek. "I need you."

She laughed and, for a moment, was tempted to stay—but she knew better. "Yes—but you don't need me right now. You need to practice."

Reed crinkled his nose, the way he always did when he was surprised. "You know what?"

"What?"

His answer was a kiss.

Beth left—reluctantly—and wandered through the cavernous lobby, barely noticing the people she passed by. She still saw Reed's face in front of her, looking at her like she could do no wrong. He was the first person she'd ever been with who didn't judge, didn't impose, didn't expect. It wasn't even that he wanted her to be happy—which was something she couldn't do, not even for him—it was enough that she did what she wanted, and that she wanted to be with him.

It made her feel like a fraud. She could hear the clock ticking in the back of her mind, and time was running out. Eventually, she would be exposed. When his arms were around her, she could relax. But every time she left his side, the fear descended like a black curtain. Would he be there when she came back?

She knew it was crazy to wonder.

But maybe it was even crazier not to prepare herself for the inevitable. Because one day, he wouldn't.

She needed some fresh air. But the hotel was like a maze, hallways leading to stairways leading to more hallways, all of which seemed to lead directly back to the gaping mouth of the casino.

"Didn't think you were the gambling type," someone said from behind her.

She didn't have to turn around to put a face to the voice—and didn't *want* to turn around, since it was a face she never wanted to see again.

"Of course, I didn't think you were the druggie type either, not after that whole Just Say No lecture on New Year's Eve," Kane sneered. "So I guess nothing should surprise me now."

Beth braced herself for attack. Since their breakup several months before, she and Kane had been at war—and things had only gotten worse since Kaia's accident. He always looked at her suspiciously, as if he could see her guilt. So, just in case, she tried not to look at him at all. "Leave me alone, Kane," she said wearily. "I'm not in the mood."

"Maybe I can help with that." Until he spoke, she hadn't even noticed the guy standing next to Kane. Maybe because he looked about as un-Kane-like as you could get, from his baggy patchwork jeans to the henna tattoo crawling across his neck. "Guaranteed mood enhancement," the guy said, handing her a chocolate bar. "Instant happiness, or your money back."

It would take more than chocolate to guarantee her happiness, especially with Kane on the prowl. Beth waved the candy away. "Thanks, but—"

"Don't waste your time," Kane sneered. "She's morally opposed to . . . well, pretty much all of life's pleasure's, wouldn't you say?"

The guy pressed the candy bar into her hand and wrapped her fingers around it, holding on for several moments too long. "I'm sure that's not true," he said, and something about his tone made Beth uneasy. She pulled her hand away.

"No, it's true," she assured him. "Kane's right. You're always right, aren't you?" she asked, aiming for sarcasm but achieving only fear.

"I was wrong about *you*," he pointed out.

Not wrong enough. He'd been right to think that she was naive enough, stupid enough to fall for his sympathetic act, straight into his arms. And he'd been right to think that he could string her along for weeks, charming her with smiles and kisses and extravagant gifts and suckering her into trusting him.

He'd just been wrong to think that when the truth came out, she'd slink away peacefully, never to be heard from again.

"Turns out this little holier-than-thou act is just a pose," Kane said. "Turns out she's just as selfish, weak, and indulgent as the rest of us—she's just not as good at it."

Beth thought about her single-minded pursuit of revenge against the people who'd ruined her life: Harper. Kane. Adam. Kaia. She'd indulged her rage, overruled the weak protests of her conscience, selfishly ignored the consequences. She'd done it all incompetently—and someone had died.

Kane didn't know it, but he was right yet again.

Reed wished he hadn't let her leave. The music still sucked, Fish and Hale still bugged—nothing was different without her there.

Except him, and not for the better.

He let Fish and Hale take off, and then he wandered off, half hoping he would find her, knowing it was unlikely. There were too many people, a crowd of strangers crushing past him. And she wasn't answering her cell.

Eventually Reed headed back to the practice room, knowing she would show up eventually. And for a second, when he opened the door and saw a figure inside cleaning things up, he thought he wouldn't have to wait.

Then he took in the dark dreads, the tattoo, the wicked smile. "Hey, Star*la," he said, leaning in the doorway. "Thanks again for the space."

"You remembered." She turned to face him, and caught him staring at the pale purple snake tattoo that twisted around her waist and climbed upward, disappearing beneath the tight black shirt.

"Tough to forget a name like that," Reed told her, his face growing a little warm. Did she realize that they didn't make girls like her back home? That if someone had asked him, last year, to describe his ideal woman, she would have looked like the front-woman of some rock funk punk band, moved like someone born onstage, spoke like music was pounding in her brain, and smiled like she knew a secret that was too good not to spill and too dangerous not to keep?

He'd thought girls like that only existed in magazines and wannabe rock star fantasies. But here she was, in the tattoo-covered, multipierced flesh.

It didn't matter what he'd wanted a year ago, he reminded himself. He'd been a kid, and now . . . a lot had changed.

But it didn't stop him from staring at her as if she were some mythical creature he'd brought to life with the power of his mind. Maybe anything was possible. Dragons. Giants. Centaurs.

And Star*las.

"I was looking for you, actually," Star*la said.

"Yeah?" Had his voice just cracked? She was surely only a year or two older than him; but he suddenly felt like he was thirteen again, covered in zits and begging his father for a real guitar.

"I just downloaded this new song and I thought you might like it," she said.

"Why?" Shit, that was rude. "I mean, what made you think that I'd . . . ?"

"I was standing outside listening to you guys practice. Does that bother you?" she asked defiantly.

Only because they sucked. "Whatever. What did you think?" Bad idea, he told himself. This girl was obviously totally into the music scene here—and *here* was about as far as you could get from home, where the Blind Monkeys were the only rock band in thirty miles, which meant they played every gig from birthday parties to funerals, despite their general level of suckitude. Star*la, clearly, would have higher standards.

She laughed. "I *thought* you might like this song I just downloaded. So . . . wanna hear it?" She pulled an iPod Nano out of her pocket—exactly the model he'd been craving but couldn't afford, not when all his extra cash went to fixing the van and helping his dad with the never-ending stack of bills.

Reed nodded, not wanting to risk another humiliating falsetto moment. He reached out for the iPod, but instead she just gave him one earbud and stuck the other in her own ear. Tethered together, they sat down on the floor, backs pressed against the wall, legs pulled up to their chests, and arms just barely touching. She pressed play.

A scorching chord blasted through the buds. A sharp, syncopated beat charged after it, overlain by a twangy acoustic guitar solo—and then, without warning, the band plugged in. And the song took off. Reed closed his eyes, letting the music storm through him, banging his head lightly back against the wall in time with the drums, his fingers flickering as if plucking and strumming invisible strings.

Everything disappeared but the music—and then the music stopped.

The first thing he registered, as the song came to an end: He and Star*la had leaned in toward each other, their cheeks and temples pressing together as they lost themselves in sound.

The second thing: Beth's face in the doorway.

She just looked lost.

chapter

5

"We're going to die." Harper gripped the bar until her knuckles turned white. One loose screw was all it would take to send her plummeting. She looked down—despite every instinct in her body screaming not to. The people were the size of pinheads. She wondered which one she would land on. "We are *so* going to die."

"It's just a ride," Adam pointed out, stretching back in the roller-coaster seat as if it were a lounge chair and grinning up at the sky. (The clouds seemed—to Harper, at least—unnaturally close.) "Enjoy it."

"I was enjoying standing flat on the ground," Harper snapped, as the car continued its slow, terrifying creep up the track. They were tilted back at nearly a right angle, and the ascent seemed to last forever. Which would have been okay with Harper, except for one little problem: What goes up, must come down. Fast. "I was enjoying the view from nine hundred feet up without feeling the asinine desire to get on a *roller coaster* that some *idiot*

thought it would be neat to build on top of a building."
She closed her eyes.

"You're the one who wanted to suck up to the girl at
the controls," Adam pointed out.

"How are we supposed to suck up to her from here?"
Harper shot back. "How are we supposed to enjoy a concert
when we're splattered on the ground a thousand feet down?"

"Why do you always have to look on the dark side of
everything?" Adam complained.

"Why do you have to act like everything's a game?
Some things aren't fun."

"*I'm* having fun," Adam countered.

"And that's all that counts?" Harper asked.

"*You're* going to lecture *me* about being self-centered?"

"I'm—" Harper's next words flew out of her mouth
and her mind as the cars rolled over the peak of the incline
and . . .

"*Aaaaaaaaaah!*" she shrieked as they whipped through
the air, the wind slicing her cheeks and her head pressed
back flat against the seat. They zoomed down the track, up
a hill, around a loop, the sky beneath her and the ground
above, her hair flying everywhere and her stomach knocking around, banging her intestines, crushing her lungs. She
kept her eyes squeezed shut and screamed and screamed,
waiting for the nightmare to end until, with a heart-
stopping jolt, it did.

Harper took a deep breath, then another. "Are we
alive?" she whispered, her eyes still shut tight.

"You were really scared, weren't you?" Adam said, and
she could hear the surprise in his voice. She would have
shot back some snide comment about how he might have

picked up on that from the hundred times she'd said it, back when he was dragging her into the seat. But she didn't have the energy. She was too relieved that it was over, and they were still alive.

There was nothing fun about screaming metal, uncontrollable speed, spinning and plunging and waiting for the crash.

At least, not when you'd been through the real thing.

Harper realized that her hands were still gripping the thin metal bar, and they weren't alone. Adam's left hand was wrapped over the top of her right one, his grip warm and firm, as if he'd meant to keep her safe.

He let go first.

"Here at Heavenly Helpers, it's all about *you,*" the attendant had chirped. "What *you* want, what *you* need, whatever makes *you* happy."

It had, in fact, sounded a bit like heaven to Miranda, whose life was usually all about anyone and everyone else. But the spa's slogan soon proved more fiction than fact, since whatever made Miranda happy most definitely did *not* include the Heavenly Peace Floral Skin Resurfacing and Pore Varnish facial.

"For your skin, dear," the woman had chirped as she slapped and pulled Miranda's face, then rubbed on a layer of acidic slime, ignoring Miranda's protestations. "Those pores are enormous, and caked with bacteria—when was your last facial?"

How about never?

Nor would she have chosen the Warming Stone Mint Massage with Body Wrap.

"It's a must!" The burly male masseur said, bustling her off to the steam room after a painful and slightly embarrassing hour of rubbing, pinching, and moisturizing. "The heat and the aromatherapy will fuse together in a blessed blend of healing vapors. It's unforgettable!"

But as far as Miranda was concerned, it was just hot and boring. And when she emerged, still covered in a thin film of all-organic mint-infused mud and smelling like a bag of potpourri, she felt neither relaxed nor rejuvenated. She just felt slimy.

"Isn't this heavenly?" the woman to her left asked, as they lay back on over-padded chairs, cucumbers covering their eyes and gauzy netting draped down over their bodies as if to protect them from mosquito sized bad karma.

"Mmm-hmmm," Miranda mumbled, trying not to seem ungrateful for her birthday present, even though the stranger in the next chair obviously had no idea who Harper was or why it would matter that Miranda feigned gratitude. "It's great." She couldn't help but wonder what Harper was thinking. Didn't her best friend know her at all? Maybe, just *maybe*, if they'd done this together, they could have laughed at the manicurist's beehive hairdo and tag-team flirted with the hot masseur. But Harper apparently preferred to spend the day without her, and Miranda was left to spend her last day as a seventeen-year-old alone, getting scolded.

The manicurist scolded her for biting her nails; the facialist scolded her for poor skin hygiene; the masseur scolded her for letting stress build up in her muscles and tie knots in her back.

Try living my life, she'd wanted to tell him. *And then talk to me about stress management.*

"My sister and I come here every year," the woman confided. "Our husbands go off and gamble or"—she tittered— "at least that's what they tell us we're doing. And we come here. It's a tradition—we've been doing it for years."

"Mmm-hmmm," Miranda mumbled again, wondering how she was supposed to relax when they stuck her in the relaxation room with someone who wouldn't leave her alone.

"Who are you here with, dear?" the woman asked.

The door opened before Miranda was forced to admit the truth: She was alone.

"Miranda Stevens?" a scratchy voice called out. "Time for your wax."

Miranda sat up and peeled the cucumber slices off her eyes, delighted to be leaving the so-called soothing sounds of the rain forest and her Chatty Cathy meditation-mate. Delighted, that is, until the woman's words sunk in. She'd seen "bikini wax" on the schedule the spa had handed her when she first walked in. But she'd elected to ignore it. She'd never had one before, and would have been more than happy to leave it at that.

But that wasn't the kind of happiness the Heavenly Helpers were shooting for.

"Nonsense," the attendant told Miranda when she tried to talk her way out of the appointment. "It's very freeing. And your boyfriend will love it."

Miranda was all for the "if you build it, he will come" theory of boyfriend hunting, but as far as she was concerned, that applied to things like chic hairstyles and sexy miniskirts.

A freshly waxed bikini line wouldn't turn her into much of an irresistible draw unless she started parading around town in a bikini . . . in which case, unwanted hair would be the least of her concerns.

Still, she lay down on the table, as the waxer insisted, wearing only her bra and underwear and feeling strangely like she was at the doctor: chilly, exposed, vulnerable, and slightly bored.

The attendant approached carrying a long strip and a brush dripping with wax, then stared down at Miranda with disdain. "You'll have to take those off," she said.

"Take what off?" There wasn't much to choose from. She pointed at her bra. "You mean . . ."

"No." The attendant scowled, as if she had better things to do than waste her time with wax neophytes who didn't know the dress code. She pointed down at Miranda's pale blue bikini briefs. "You're blocking my access."

"But they're bikini," Miranda protested. "So it should be—"

"We do *Brazilian* waxes here," the woman informed her. In the midst of her confusion, Miranda noted that the waxer could use some wax herself on her upper lip; she decided not to mention it.

"I don't . . . is that some special type of . . . ?"

The woman rolled her eyes. "We wax it all, honey. We leave you completely bare."

"*Completely* . . . bare?" Miranda repeated, understanding dawning over her, swiftly followed by horror.

"Completely bare. Down there."

And that's when Miranda got the hell out.

"You guys have a fun ride?" Carl's friend Esther gave her replacement a quick wave and laced her arms through Harper's and Adam's, leading them to the opposite end of the roof.

"I did," Adam began, "but I think Harper—"

"It was great," Harper cut in. "Thanks so much for the free ride. Adam was just—"

"Thought his name was Kane?" Esther cut in.

"It is," Harper said quickly. "Adam's just his middle name. I call him that to bug him. Uh . . . anyway, he was just telling me how grateful he was for the free ride. Weren't you?" She glared at him, as if he was failing to get the message.

Which, apparently, he was, because Adam had no idea what he was supposed to say next. "Um, yeah, thanks. It was great."

"Cool." Esther pulled out a pack of cigarettes. She took one out, then tipped the pack toward Harper and Adam, who both shook their heads. Shrugging, she hunched over, trying to protect her lighter from the wind. "I hate it up here," she complained. "It takes the whole damn break to light the thing up," she complained.

"Adam can help you," Harper said quickly.

I can? Adam mouthed. Harper just grabbed the lighter and tossed it to him and, with luck, he got the flame lit and held it to Esther's cigarette.

She leaned against the railing, tipped her head back, and sucked in one long drag, then another. Finally, she seemed to remember she wasn't alone. "So, Carl sent you?" Esther asked. She gave Adam an appraising look, then grinned. "Lucky me."

Adam had been off the dating market for a while, but

he knew flirting when he saw it. Harper's expression remained neutral, as if she hadn't noticed—or didn't care.

"So what can I do for you?" Esther asked.

Adam waited for Harper to speak, but when she didn't, he stepped in. "Well, this is a little awkward, but—"

"Just tell her," Harper said quickly. She gave Esther a half smile. "He can be a little shy, especially around cute girls."

What? Before he could say anything, Harper gave him the signal they'd used when they were kids whenever an intruder had walked in on one of their clubhouse meetings (membership was exclusive, limited to Harper and Adam). She made a fist with her right hand and, tucking her fingers under her chin, pressed her thumb to her lips. Meaning: *Shut the hell up. Now.*

Esther fluffed her hair out and tipped her head to one side. "So you think I'm cute?" She ran her hand lightly across Adam's bicep. "You're not too bad yourself."

Adam got the plan: Flirt with her, charm her, then get the tickets out of her. And given Esther's long, tan legs peeking out from beneath her short sundress, her pert nose, big brown eyes, and full lips, the mission shouldn't have been much of a burden.

But it still felt like one. Not because he wasn't attracted to her, and not because he felt guilty—just because he didn't feel like flirting.

He would do it, anyway, for Harper.

"Esther's a great name," he said, the best he could come up with on short notice. "It's unusual. But really pretty."

She shrugged. "It's my grandmother's," she said. "Most of my friends call me Estie."

Adam flashed a grin. "Okay, *Estie*. So, say I just got into town and I'm looking for something fun to do—any recommendations?"

"Why recommend when I could show?" she asked, stepping forward and looping an arm around Adam's shoulder. "Where should we go first?"

"Uh, don't you have to work?" Harper asked, sounding a little cranky.

"I can switch shifts," Estie said. "It's not every day that a guy this cute walks into my life." She tousled Adam's hair, and he squirmed away. "Aw, he *is* shy, just like you said. So adorable!"

"Yeah. Adorable," Harper muttered. "The thing is, we've got stuff to do—"

"We're on vacation," Adam pointed out. "We've got plenty of time. So, Estie, where shall we go?"

"The gondola rides at the Venetian are über-romantic," she told him, then frowned at Harper. "They only seat two, though, so you should probably stay here. It was nice to meet you, though. Come on, Adam—Kane—whoever you are."

Estie grabbed Adam's hand and began tugging him toward the elevator doors. He gave Harper a helpless look, then followed.

Harper didn't look in the mood to help; she looked in the mood to attack. "No!" Estie and Adam froze. "He can't go with you."

"He can't?"

"I can't?"

"And why not?" Estie asked.

"Because he's—we're—he was just—you just can't,"

she sputtered, slapping the railing for emphasis. "Just tell her you have to *go*."

Estie burst into laughter. "That took longer than I thought," she exclaimed.

"What?" Harper and Adam asked together, completely confused.

"Carl called me to tell me you guys were coming over here, and that you were looking for Crash Burners tickets," Estie admitted. "Trying to flirt them out of me?" She shook her head at Adam. "That's low."

Harper sagged back against the railing, looking half relieved and half humiliated. Adam was still just confused. "How did you know that's what I was trying to do?" His flirting skills had never let him down in the past—but maybe it *wasn't* like riding a bicycle, after all.

"Come on, you guys are obviously together."

Adam and Harper just looked at each other, then back at Estie. "Us?" Adam asked incredulously. "Did Carl tell you that?"

"No, it's just obvious," Estie said. "You are, aren't you?"

Adam wondered which part of the hostile, nonstop bickering, no-touching interactions between him and Harper could have screamed "relationship."

"Definitely not," he said firmly. "No way."

"Seriously?" Estie looked back and forth between the two of them. "Well, then, you should be."

Adam laughed—and then, too late, caught the look on Harper's face. He wanted to apologize; he hadn't been laughing at the idea of the two of them together. It was just the whole awkward, painful, utterly ridiculous situation. But he couldn't say any of that in front of a stranger. And even if he'd been alone, he suspected he couldn't have explained it, anyway. He wouldn't have known how.

"Man, I was so sure there was something between you guys," Estie said.

Harper looked over the railing, out at the sprawling strip of lights and people far beneath them. "Trust me," she said in a flat voice. "You couldn't be more wrong."

"That's my final offer," Kane said firmly. "Take it or—"

"I'll take it." Jackson, who'd proved a shrewder negotiator than Kane had expected, extended his hand, then whipped it away again just as Kane was about to shake. "On one condition."

"Try me." The price was right, the wrappers were flawless, and there was no way Kane was going to screw up his first big deal.

"Hook me up with your hot, blond friend."

Kane let out a whoosh of air. He wanted to say yes. He would have *loved* to say yes, for more reasons than one. But . . .

"No can do." Kane slumped down on one of the lobby chairs. "In case you didn't notice, she hates me."

Jackson nodded and raised his eyebrows. "That's what made her so hot. Spicy food and spicy women—that's what it's all about, am I right?"

Being so close to a black hole of classlessness made Kane's skin crawl. But his facade—smooth, polite, mildly bored, and immune to shock—was well worn and impossible to shake. "You know it," he agreed, baring his teeth in the imitation of a smile. "But Beth's about as spicy as vanilla pudding. You wouldn't be interested. Trust me."

"And you know this because . . . ?"

"Let's just say, been there, done that." Kane winced at the sleaze, but pushed on. "If you know what I mean."

"Really?" Jackson's eyes widened, and he held out his palm for Kane to slap. *"Nice."*

"Not really," Kane said wryly. "So do we have a deal?"

"I don't know." Jackson laced his fingers together and stretched his arms out in front of him, a yawn contorting his face. "I was really counting on Barbie to sweeten the pot. Now, I don't know . . ."

"Wait. You say you like bitter, argumentative girls?" He was getting an idea. He didn't much like it, but that didn't keep him from recognizing its genius.

"You know it," Jackson said eagerly, leaning forward. "You got someone else?"

"How do you feel about sarcasm?"

"Love it."

"How about pessimism?" Kane continued.

"Hot."

"Insults? Arguments? The burning need to always get the last word?"

Jackson rubbed his palms together. "Bring it on. So what's she look like?"

Kane wasn't the type to grapple with indecision. He usually knocked it out in a single punch and vaulted right over it. But this time, something made him pause, at least for a moment.

But it was no more than that.

"Well, let me ask you this," he finally said, a plan coalescing. "How do you feel about redheads?"

❖❖❖

"Excrement."

"Simply awful."

"The worst I've ever seen."

"You should sue your guitar teacher for criminal incompetence."

Beth cringed at every word out of the judges' mouths. Reed, Fish, and Hale, on the other hand, stood lined up at the edge of the stage, taking it all without a single change in facial expression. Beth knew that, were she up there, listening to a panel of so-called experts bash her talent and smash her dreams, she'd be a wreck. In tears, inconsolable; but Reed looked as if he was barely listening, and the other two followed his cue.

The All-American Band Battle had introduced a new judging tactic this year—if you could call a total rip-off of a played-out reality TV show "new." The organizers had assembled a team of experts—the Gee Whiz Kids, a pop foursome with pseudo-indie cred and a cult following, in town to open for the Crash Burners—and given them free reign to bash the bands in front of the audience. Beth had been watching for an hour and she had yet to see the panel give anyone a thumbs up. That said, she'd also not seen a single band come in for the beating that the Blind Monkeys were taking. Not even close.

"Can you even call that music?" asked one of the Gee Whiz Kids who—certainly to the delight of the organizers—had a possibly authentic British accent. "Because I call it noise, plain and simple."

"And the song? What *was* that?" another asked. "No, really, I'm asking—you, lead singer guy, where the hell did you get that?"

Reed leaned into the mic. "I wrote it," he said, looking out into the audience and meeting Beth's eyes. She knew the lyrics by heart:

> *I don't know where you are,*
> *but I'm there with you.*
> *Your lips, your tongue, your fire*
> *It's all I wanna do . . .*

She'd often wondered whether he had written it about her—for her—but she'd never had the nerve to ask. Still, the song was one of her favorites.

"It's rubbish," the vaguely British guy snapped, dismissing it with a wave of his hand. "Pointless lyrics, bad rhymes, sappy sentiment. This isn't nursery school."

"And it's not a karaoke bar!" one of the other judges chimed in; he'd used the same line on almost every band. Apparently, he thought it quite clever. So did Beth . . . or at least she had, the first time she'd heard it, back before Simon Cowell had stopped recycling put-downs. A million times later, with the phrase spilling from the mouth of an already washed-up wannabe, and aimed at her boyfriend, she was less than amused.

"Judges?" British guy asked, turning to face the panel. "What do you say?" By the rules of the competition, the four of them would now vote on whether to pass the Blind Monkeys on to the next round or eject them from the competition. Beth wasn't waiting on the edge of her seat.

Judge #1: "They're out."

Judge #2: "So far out, they're almost in again . . . but, not."

Hilarious, Beth thought. *Somebody get this guy on* Letterman.

Judge #3: "Out. Go find a karaoke bar and leave us alone."

Judge #4, with a smart British lilt that gave Beth a serious case of déjà vu: "Out. Best of luck, fellows. You're going to need it."

As the guys filed offstage, Beth rushed out of the auditorium and hurried to meet them at the stage door. Her heart ached for Reed. She just wanted to find him, comfort him, fix him. Strong as he was, he couldn't have escaped something like that without breaking. He had comforted her so many times, mostly without even knowing why, and without asking. He would just let her cry in his arms, clinging to him, unable to tell him the reason for fear it would drive him away.

He never seemed to need her, not the way she needed him. But maybe now she could pay him back.

Not that she was glad, she told herself. Not that she would ever want him to fail. She just wanted her chance to prove how much she cared about him—and this was it. She would reassure him that *she* knew he was amazing, no matter what anyone else thought.

And they would both remember that he needed her too.

"I'm so sorry!" she cried, as soon as he emerged from backstage. Fish and Hale followed behind, laughing—Beth wasn't surprised. They had no ambition; there was nothing to be crushed. But Reed looked even paler than usual, drawn into himself. "You were so amazing. I don't know what they were talking about."

She tried to hug him, but he neatly sidestepped her.

"They were right," he said in a hollow, wooden voice. "We played like ass. And the song—"

"I love that song," she assured him, compromising by stepping behind him and putting her arms around his waist, pressing her head against his shoulder blades.

"It's crap."

"No—"

"Beth. Just—" He pulled her arms apart and stepped away. "Just let it go. It's fine. They were right. I'm over it."

"Reed . . ." She wanted to touch him again, to remind him that she was there—that he wanted her there—but forced herself not to push. "It's just one opinion."

"Actually, it's four." His laugh was short and off-key.

"Maybe it was just—"

"Yo, tough break." Star★la rounded the corner and gave Reed a sympathetic punch on the shoulder. She waved at the guys, but didn't acknowledge Beth.

"You were watching?" Reed's voice shot to a higher octave and, though it might have been Beth's imagination, he seemed to stand slightly straighter. Taller. "We were playing like shit today."

Beth put her hand on his shoulder. "No you—"

"Yeah," Star★la interrupted. "It happens. But the song's not bad—ever think about switching it up in the bridge, have your drummer shift to 4/4 and then maybe jumping a key?"

To Beth, it all sounded like a foreign language. But Reed suddenly brightened up. "That's not bad," he mused. "Fish, you get that?"

"Yeah, I heard. Could work."

"And I was thinking, maybe in that first verse . . ."

Beth tuned out. She stared at the floor. Counted the lights in the ceiling. Tried not to notice that Reed and Star★la looked like a matching pair in their vintage tees and black denim, while Beth looked like a refugee from a J. Crew clearance sale. She'd always thought that belly button piercings looked kind of slutty, but on Star★la . . . well, slutty, yes. But she couldn't help notice that Reed's eyes kept dropping down to the glint of silver that poked out above her low-riding jeans. *Stop worrying,* she told herself. *Reed isn't Adam. He would never . . .*

She didn't even want to put it into words, because that might make it real.

"Beth, sound okay to you?"

"What?" He was looking at her again, waiting for an answer. But to what?

"Star★la's done here and she says she can show us some bar downtown where all the locals hang out. You want to?" Reed had never expected anything from her before, but now it was clear: He expected an answer, and he expected it to be a yes.

"I don't have my ID on me," she said hesitantly, thankful that it was true.

"No problem." Star★la grinned. "This isn't an ID kind of place. You'll see."

"Beth?" Reed curled his arm around her waist and tugged her toward him. "If you don't want to, we don't have to, but . . ."

"No. Sounds great," she said, hoping she seemed sincere. She'd wanted to help him, and if this is what it took to cheer him up—if *Star★la* cheered him up, with her stupid piercings and her tattoos and her oh-so-happening bar scene—then that's what it took. Tonight wasn't about Beth; it was about Reed. She had no reason to feel threatened, she reminded herself. And even if she did, she wasn't going to let that stand in his way.

chapter

6

They strode up to the hotel check-in desk hand in hand, identical love-struck smiles painted on their faces. "This is a bad idea," Adam muttered out of the side of his mouth, trying not to let the happy expression falter.

"It's our best shot," Harper countered, through gritted teeth. "Just act happy."

"I'm not that good an actor."

Estie hadn't been able to help them with the concert tickets, but she had offered them a lead: The hotel that was hosting the concert often reserved a few free event passes for especially cute honeymooners.

So here they were, glowing with fake love and walking on artificial sunshine. A chipper brunette named Margie— at least, according to her I'M MARGIE, TELL ME HOW I CAN HELP name tag—greeted them at the desk.

"Yes?" she asked.

They'd agreed it would be best not to come right out and ask for the tickets, at least not at first. Better to be so insufferably adorable that Margie had no choice but to reward them.

"We just wanted to thank y'all for letting us stay in your lovely hotel on our special weekend," Harper said, the Southern accent pouring out before she realized what she was doing. "Sweetie pie here is just loving every minute of it." She nuzzled her face into Adam's neck—pausing for a moment to enjoy the familiar scent, woodsy and clean. It had been so long since they'd . . .

No. This was no time for sappy love-struck nostalgia: It was a time for romance.

"I could just take you back to the room right now," she murmured, then turned back to Margie, confiding, "We've barely left the room all weekend. You know how it is."

The look on Margie's face said no, she didn't know how it was, nor did she want to. "Glad you're enjoying your stay with us," she said tentatively. "So this is a special weekend for you?"

"Me and the wife just got hitched!" Adam said, lifting Harper up and whirling her around. "She's my wife! Woo!"

Harper resisted the urge to smack him. She'd said act cute, adorable—not wasted. He was acting like he was at a tailgate party. Though she had to admit, it was indeed pretty damn cute.

"So, newlyweds," Margie said, sounding less than enthused. "Congratulations."

Harper gave Adam a quick kiss on the cheek. "I wanted a simple church wedding, back home, but my man here, he's just obsessed."

"Obsessed?" Adam and Margie asked together.

"With Elvis. So of course we just had to come to Vegas

and get hitched at the Hunka Hunka Chapel of Love, and you"—she dug her finger gently into Adam's chest— "looked so handsome in your white jumpsuit and those sexy sunglasses."

"Well, uh"—Adam gave her his best Elvis lip-curl— "thank you, thank you very much." Beneath the counter, Adam gave Harper a quick pinch just above the hip, and she bit her lip to keep from squealing. He knew that was where she was most ticklish; he was *trying* to make her laugh. It wasn't going to work. "I'm just sorry about last night," he said.

"Uh, last night?"

"You know." He lowered his voice to a stage whisper. "When we were in bed and . . . I called you *Priscilla*."

Now Harper nearly did laugh. But, instead, she gave him a light slap across the face. "You're going to bring that up in front of a stranger?" she cried. "You *know* I'll never be able to measure up to her. I try and I try, I got the implants and the new hairdo and—"

"Give it a rest, guys," Margie snapped, the help-me-help-you grin gone from her face.

"What?" Harper asked, trying to look innocent.

"You heard about the free tickets for newlyweds, right? You think you're the first couple to try this?" She rolled her eyes. "You're just the worst."

Harper glanced at Adam, briefly considered trying to bluff it out, then shrugged in defeat. "So much for my acting career." She hoped she sounded sufficiently breezy. It wouldn't do to let either of them know how much she'd been counting on these tickets—how she'd decided that one grand gesture for Miranda would, just maybe, erase everything Harper had done to her this year, and let them start fresh. And more than that—chasing down the tickets had helped distract her from thing things that actually mattered. But that was over now.

She tugged at Adam's shirt. "Come on, let's get out of here."

He shook her off and planted his hands on the fake wooden desk. "Isn't there anything you can do?"

Margie blew out an exasperated sigh. "I don't have time for this. Come on, listen to your girlfriend—give up."

And for a moment, Adam looked like he was considering it. Then his jaw tightened—it was so imperceptible that someone else might not have noticed. But Harper knew what to watch for. And she was always watching.

"I know you're busy," Adam said. "I know you don't have time for a couple of high school kids trying to score free tickets. But just listen to me. We need this. *She* needs this." Harper froze, but he didn't try to touch her, or even look at her. "And it's none of your business why, so you're just going to have to trust me. She has gone through way more shit this year than anyone should ever have to, and I'm not saying she can't take it, because she can, and she *has*, and she doesn't complain, and she never asks for help and—" He paused, and took a deep breath, then another, and when he spoke again, his voice had lost some of its volume, but none of its intensity. "And now she's asking for this one thing," he said slowly. "And I wish I could give it to her. I really wish—" Harper was staring at the ground, but she could feel him watching her. "But I can't. *You* can. Please."

Margie tore herself away from Adam's face and looked over at Harper, who forced herself to meet her gaze. *Do not cry,* she commanded herself. She refused to be pitied, not by some random hotel clerk, not by Adam, not by anyone. *Just breathe.*

Finally, Margie's expression softened and she nodded. "I'm not supposed to do this, but . . ."

Adam snatched the tickets out of her hand and passed them to Harper, who stayed still and silent, just focusing on keeping her composure.

Adam pulled her away, and they walked through the lobby in silence. Finally, outside the hotel, Harper stopped. "Adam, I . . ." She chewed on the inside of her cheek, trying to figure out how to say what she wanted to say—how to thank him for helping her, despite the way she'd treated him, despite what she'd done to him, despite everything. She glanced down at the tickets, still unable to believe that they'd actually, finally succeeded. "Adam, I just want to say—holy shit!"

"What?"

Without a word, she handed him one of the tickets. He looked down, then back up at her, his mouth a perfect O of horror.

Margie had scored them second-row seats to a one night only, sold-out concert:

The Ninth Annual Viva Las Vegas International Elvis Extravaganza.

Thank you, Margie. Thank you very much.

If there had been papers, they would have been signed, sealed, and delivered. But this was a handshake business, and hands had been shook. As Kane led Jackson through the Camelot's lobby in search of the pool—in search of

Miranda, who'd been only too happy to agree to meet him and his "friend"—Kane couldn't help but feel extremely pleased with himself. Even more than usual.

He'd suckered Jackson into agreeing to the deal, for the sole concession of introducing him to a hot redhead—an introduction, and nothing more. After that, they were on their own. So it wasn't like he was selling out Miranda, he told himself. More like he was using her as bait—bait that was in no danger of even a nibble, since obviously once Jackson saw her, the whole sordid business would be over with. Not that Miranda was some kind of guy repellant. But Jackson wasn't going to waste his Vegas weekend on a mousy, bookish stringbean, no matter how entertaining, and Kane doubted whether Miranda would last more than ten minutes with the smooth-talking, peace-loving, hemp-weaving Jackson before getting up and out.

No harm, no foul, and plenty of money soon to be rolling in. All in all, Kane decided, a good day's work.

"So how do I get in good with this chick?" Jackson asked, as they stepped onto the pool deck.

Calling her *chick* would surely be a great place to start, Kane thought in amusement. This could be more fun than he'd thought.

The pool area was mostly empty. A few kids were playing Marco Polo in the shallow end, splashing and screaming. Kane caught one kid cheating—climbing out of the pool and running to the other end before diving back in, just as he was about to get tagged. Underhanded—and brilliant. It brought back fond memories.

"I don't see her," he said, wondering if it had taken her longer to get back from the spa than she'd expected. His gaze skimmed across a row of women lying in the shade: old lady with her knitting, desperate housewife with curves several sizes bigger than her suit, skinny twelve-year-old trying to look like Britney, and . . . whoa. Kane nodded appreciatively and drank in a pair of perfect, delicate feet, each toe painted a deep shade of red, slim, pale legs, lime green bikini board shorts, a flat, taut midriff and barely there bikini top and—

Their eyes met, and she propped herself up and waved.

"Tell me that's your redhead," Jackson said in a hushed voice.

Kane could hardly believe it, but . . . "Yeah. That's Miranda."

Jackson slapped him on the back. "Nice, dude. I knew I had a good feeling about you. Let's do this."

Kane led Jackson over and they sat down on an adjacent chair. He couldn't stop staring: Everything about her looked the same as always. She was still just Miranda—but looking at her from across the pool, as if she were a stranger, it had been . . . deeply weird. He tried to shake it off. Bikini or not, pedicure or not, sexy half smile or not, this was still Miranda. *Just* Miranda.

"Stevens, I'd like you to meet a good friend of mine," he said as she set down her book and extended a hand.

"*You* can call me Miranda," she told the drug dealer, touching her face self-consciously. Her skin looked almost like it was glowing.

"Jackson," he said, shaking her hand. The dealer checked out her book. "*Anna Karenina*?" he asked, raising his eyebrows. "Not quite beach reading."

Miranda waved her hand toward the giant waterslide

and the plastic palm trees. "Not quite the beach," she pointed out.

"It's one of my favorites," Jackson told her. "I love the way Tolstoy uses the theme of the moving train to propel us through the book."

"Really?" Miranda asked, her eyes widening in surprise.

"Really?" Kane echoed. What was going on here?

Jackson began explaining his take on Tolstoy and why he preferred him to Dostoyevsky ("*Crime and Punishment* is thought-provoking, to be sure, but *War and Peace* changed my life. . . .") but liked Chekhov best of all, especially on his "dark days." Miranda listened in rapt amazement.

Kane couldn't bring himself to listen at all. Nor did he pay much attention when Miranda offered her own criticisms of the novel and then shifted from fiction to current events, analyzing the latest move by the Russian president, while Jackson jumped in with a comparison to nineteenth-century geopolitics. Instead, Kane watched. He watched Miranda nervously play with her hands, picking at her cuticles with sudden, sneaky plucks as if no one could see. He noticed her smoothing down her hair and grazing her fingers across her lips, and he noted that when Jackson made her laugh, he briefly rested his hand on her skin—first on her arm, then on her thigh. Kane spotted her blushing, and caught Jackson sneaking more than one glance at the low neckline of the bikini, always darting his eyes back up to Miranda's before she picked up on his distraction.

And finally, he couldn't take it anymore.

"Jackson, can I talk to you for a minute?" he asked.

"Kinda busy here," Jackson said, without turning his gaze from Miranda.

"It's important." Kane stood up and waited for Jackson to follow. "We'll be back in one minute, Stevens. Promise." He pulled Jackson across the deck to the other side of the pool, where the Marco Polo game had morphed into netless water volleyball. "What are you doing?" he hissed.

"Reeling in the catch of the day," Jackson leered. "You were right, she's as spicy as they come."

Kane winced. This had to be handled delicately—but it had to be handled. "But all that stuff about Tolstoy, politics—where did you . . . ?"

"You gotta play to the audience," Jackson explained. "Let them think you're on the same wavelength, and then—" He shook his head. "You think all this hippie crap is my idea? My girlfriend's all peace, love, happiness, bullshit—but if it keeps her happy to dress me like granola boy, well, you do what you gotta do, am I right?"

"Your . . . girlfriend?" Kane wondered why his brain was moving so much more slowly than usual.

"Yeah, she's getting in on Monday. But till then, I figure I can have a little fun, and Miranda's perfect—or she will be, once she loosens up a little."

"Look, Jackson, I know I said she was your type, but I really don't think—"

"I owe you one," Jackson said, clapping Kane on the back. "But now, how about you get out of here and leave us to it."

Kane was stuck. He couldn't afford to alienate Jackson—but he couldn't just let Miranda walk into the lion's den wearing a necklace of raw meat.

You don't owe anything to anyone, he reminded himself.

Words to live by—words he always *had* lived by—but that didn't make them true.

The Tonky Honk was half bar, half coffeehouse, and all hipster. The nexus of the Vegas indie rock scene—at least, according to Star*la, a self-described expert—it was packed, even in the middle of the afternoon, with world-weary aspiring poets sipping anise and off-duty house bands knocking back shots. Papers lined with song lyrics and guitar chords lined the walls, a floor-to-ceiling tribute to a million impossible dreams. And, on a small stage in a dark recess of the bar, a four-piece band played inter-minable songs about flat tires and worn-out toothbrushes, each bleeding into the next in a tedious litany of trivial torments. According to Star*la, the Tonky Honk was a Vegas institution, occasionally attracting legends like Tony Bennett for a post-concert drink. (Reluctant to admit she didn't know who that was, Beth just ooh'd and aah'd along with the rest of them.)

Beth slumped in the corner of a back booth sipping a weak espresso while the guys drowned their sorrows in a seemingly bottomless bottle of whiskey. Star*la, of course, matched them drink for drink.

She was regaling them with backstage stories about a bunch of bands Beth had never heard of, all of whom had apparently passed through Vegas—and through Star*la—in the past year. Fish, Hale, and Reed couldn't get enough of it.

"So, what kind of stuff do you listen to?" Star*la sud-denly asked Beth.

She flushed, and tucked a lock of blond hair behind her

ear. "I, uh, you know. Whatever." She wasn't about to say the words "Tori Amos" or "Sarah McLachlan" in a place like this.

Reed nudged her. "You know you love all those weepy girls," he told her. "Dar Williams. Ani DiFranco. And, of course—"

"Let me guess," Star★la said. "Tori Amos."

Beth's face turned bright red as everyone else at the table burst into laughter. She didn't even get what was so funny—or so lame—about her taste, but that was probably part of the problem. "That's not all I like," she said defensively. She brushed some stray curls out of Reed's face. "You know I love your stuff."

Reed raised his glass in a drunken toast. "To Beth, our one and only fan!" He clinked her glass loudly, his whiskey splashing over the side and spattering into her cup.

Beth's first impulse was to comfort him; Star★la's, apparently, was to ridicule. "Is he always such a whiny baby?" she asked Beth, as if to forge some kind of sisterhood. Beth just shrugged and looked away. "You know what you need?" Star★la asked.

Reed, Hale, and Fish exchanged a glance, and then chorused, "Another drink!"

"Not quite." Star★la hopped up from the table. "Be right back." She jogged toward the bar and began an animated conversation with the bartender. The boys watched, though Beth was unsure whether they were wondering about her plan or admiring the way she filled out her jeans.

Reed's hand was resting on Beth's inner thigh, and the warm pressure on her leg should have been comforting:

He was with her, and that's all that mattered. But his mind was somewhere else.

"It's all set," Star*la said, bounding back to the table. "The guys are a little sensitive about other people touching their instruments, but they've got no problem with Reed doing it."

"With Reed doing what?" Beth asked.

"Jamming with them," Star*la explained, as if it had been obvious.

"You crazy?" Reed asked.

"Do a couple songs," she urged him. "Get back on the horse. They'll play anything you want—they know no one's listening. Hey!" she turned to Beth. "Why don't you go too?"

"Uh . . . what?" Beth cringed under Star*la's gaze, feeling herself slide down a bit in the seat and wishing she could go all the way, right under the table.

"A duet!" Star*la exclaimed. "It would be great. Like karaoke, right?"

Beth winced at the word, but the guys burst into laughter.

"Awesome!" Fish said, apparently—and unusually—not too stoned to follow along with the conversation. "Go for it."

"Yeah, man, you and your girlfriend, rocking out," Hale agreed. "That's hot."

Hale thought everything was hot.

Reed turned to her, a questioning look on his face. "It could be . . ."

"No." The word slipped out before she had a chance to think; but really, it was the only possible option. Beth didn't sing in public. She didn't even sing in the shower. Not that she had a terrible voice—but the thought of anyone hearing her sing, much less watching her stand up on a stage, under the spotlight, staring at her, judging her, laughing at her—even imagining it made her want to throw up. "I can't."

"Sure you can," Reed encouraged her. He stood up and tugged at her arm. "It'll be fun." She could tell by his glazed look and careful enunciation that he was drunk. Otherwise, she was sure, he would never push the issue. He should, by now, know her well enough to understand why going up on that stage would be a walking nightmare for her. "It'll be fun. You and me. C'mon."

"I can't sing," she protested, shaking him off.

"Anyone can sing!" He grabbed her again, pulling her out of the seat. She stumbled into his arms.

"No!" She shook him off. "I *can't!*"

"Let it go, Reed," Star★la said, touching his shoulder. "She doesn't want to." She turned toward Beth and apologized, but Beth barely heard—she was too busy wondering why a single word from Star★la had been enough to get him to stop. And wondering whether Beth had really *wanted* him to stop. Maybe if he'd kept pushing, she would have given in and followed him up to the stage. And maybe that would have been for the best. "Come on," Star★la said, guiding him away from the table. "I'll go with you."

Of course she would.

Reed took the stage and, giving a few quiet instructions to the band, leaned into the mic and began to sing. Beth expected him to do the same number the Blind Monkeys had performed that afternoon, but instead, the band launched into a Rolling Stones cover. "*When I'm driving in my car,*" Reed sang, "*and that man comes on the radio . . .*"

Beth drew in a sharp breath. It was the perfect song for him—his voice, scratchy and low, massaged the words, rising and falling with the melody, sometimes straying off the beat, forging ahead and then falling behind. She closed her eyes, letting his voice surround, drawing it inside her. He stumbled over the words and as the music swept past him, a rich, deep, *female* voice took over, picking up where he'd left off and carrying the song until Reed could join back in.

Beth opened her eyes and there they were, hunched over the microphone together, voices melding together, faces beaming, Star★la's dreads whipping through the air as she flung her head back and forth, his curls flying, their hands both gripping the mic stand, nearly touching, their bodies dancing them toward each other, then away, then back again, ever closer to embrace.

"*I can't get no, satisfaction,*" they howled, and Beth looked away, suddenly feeling like *she* was the interloper, catching the two of them in an intensely private moment, invading a closed-off world. "*'Cause I try, and I try, and I try, and I tryyyyyyyyy . . .*"

Reed would never cheat on her, but nothing he could do with Star★la behind her back would be as raw and sensual as what he was doing right now, onstage, in front of all these people, letting himself go and charging through the music, stomping with the beat, losing control, with her. Beth and Reed were never that free with each other, that close, swept away, because Beth couldn't afford to lose control. She always had to keep a piece of herself—the most important piece—locked away.

But that's just an excuse, Beth thought, placing her mug carefully on the table and standing up. Fish and Hale, mesmerized, didn't even notice. Her reluctance—her *inability*—to get up on that stage didn't have anything to do with keeping secrets. She had to admit it to herself, as she slipped quietly away from the table, moving toward the exit, knowing she wouldn't be missed. She wasn't holding herself back for the sake of caution or self-protection.

It was just fear.

"So I have to ask—what's with the tie-dye?" Miranda didn't even hesitate to say it. For some reason, nervous paranoia had yet to set in. Maybe because she was on vacation, in a strange place with a strange guy, with no baggage and no expectations for the future, nothing to risk and nothing to lose—or maybe it was just Jackson. She felt comfortable with him, free to speak her mind. It wasn't like they'd settled into some cozy conversational groove, pretending they'd known each other forever; it was more that there seemed no danger that she could say the wrong thing. She could somehow tell that he was enjoying everything that popped out of her mouth. The feeling was mutual.

He was fascinating, funny, and—once you got past the wispy goatee and overgrown hair—adorable.

"You know Berkeley." He shrugged. "It's illegal there not to wear some kind of tie-dye or peace sign on at least one part of your body."

In fact, she didn't know Berkeley—pretty much didn't

know anywhere beyond the claustrophobic confines of Grace, CA. Which was why she couldn't believe that this guy, this *college* guy, was wasting his time on her.

"Hate to mention this to you, but you're not in Berkeley anymore," she pointed out.

If this had been Kane she was talking to, he would have immediately wondered whether that was a veiled invitation to take his shirt off. And then he promptly would have obliged.

But it wasn't Kane—after hanging out for a few minutes he'd obviously decided he had something better to do. Jackson just plucked at the edge of the multicolored shirt. "Yeah, but it's all I've got," he said without a hint of self-consciousness. "I'm just not that into clothes. Or appearances, you know?"

Maybe that was why he was still talking to her, Miranda concluded, despite the fact that she was wearing a bikini that exposed more of her flab and cellulite than she'd ever allowed anyone to see. (She had intended to cover up before Kane and his friend arrived, determined not to let him see the humiliating bulges and sags, but—unwilling as ever to accommodate her hopes—he'd arrived early.)

"So what *are* you into?" she pressed. "Other than Tolstoy and world peace, of course."

"What am I into?" Jackson tipped his head back to catch the fading light of the afternoon sun. "The taste of cold beer at a baseball game, when the score is tied and your team has one man on base and two outs," he said. "Discovering a new band, just after they've found their sound, but before they sign away their souls to the radio gods. Poems that make no fucking sense but still manage to blow your mind. And"—he gave her a mischievous smile—"good conversation with pretty girls."

Miranda felt the heat rising to her cheeks. "In that case, what are you doing here?" she joked.

He didn't laugh. "Having an amazing afternoon," he told her, with a totally straight face.

Miranda didn't know what to make of it. A cute, smart, older guy, giving her two compliments in a row as if it was nothing? Guys her age didn't talk like that—at least, not to her.

So, instead of responding, she just laughed nervously and turned toward the pool. "The water looks so tempting when you can't go in, doesn't it?" she asked. "Even though you know it's just going to be cold and over-chlorinated, from here it looks so insanely refreshing, like we're in some kind of beer commercial."

"Who says we can't go in?" Jackson asked, appearing not to care that she'd randomly changed the subject.

"Well, I guess I *could*," Miranda allowed, though she had no intention of doing anything of the sort. "But I think you've got a small problem."

"And that would be?"

"Shirt? Jeans? Shoes? Unless you're going to dive in like this, or—" She stopped, realizing that she didn't know this guy well enough to suggest a skinny-dip, even as a joke. "I'd say swimming is out."

"You don't think I'd jump in with my clothes on?" Jackson asked.

"Now *that*, I'd love to see," Miranda said, laughing. The only people left at the pool were a few little kids and their nervous mothers, who she guessed wouldn't take too kindly to some random college student throwing himself in fully clothed. (Although this was Vegas—surely it wouldn't be the first time.)

"What do I get?" Jackson sat up and leaned forward. Their knees were almost touching.

"Get for what?"

"For jumping in the pool and soaking myself, just for your amusement," he explained, staring at her so intensely, she had to force herself not to look away.

"I don't know. A dollar?"

"How about you go out with me tonight?" he suggested, his grin stretching nearly to his ears.

"I barely know you," Miranda said, as her brain furiously tried to process the request. He wanted to go out? With her? Like, on a date? Would it *be* a date? What else could it be? "For all I know, you're some psychotic ax murderer trolling cheap hotels looking for redheads to chop up for your salad. I watch *CSI*."

"I don't think your buddy Kane would have introduced you to an ax murderer," Jackson pointed out. "And I've never seen *CSI*, but I can assure you that I'm a vegetarian. Only thing in my salad is lettuce and tofu."

She was supposed to meet up with Harper for the night—although, Miranda reminded herself, Harper had ditched her that morning and probably never looked back. And she would be the first person to urge Miranda to go on a date. She always pushed Miranda toward every guy who crossed her path—every guy, that is, except Kane. The ultimate lost cause.

Miranda had to admit that she'd been hoping to spend

the night hanging out with him—along with Harper and Adam, of course, but that was a coupling-off waiting to happen and, if it did, she'd be left alone with Kane. In a place where, according to him, anything could happen.

Anything like what? she asked herself. *What the hell am I waiting for?* Kane had, several months before, finally seen her as something more than boring Miranda, just one of the guys. He'd taken her out, he'd *kissed* her—and that had been the end of it. The moment she'd spent all those years dreaming of had come, and then gone, almost as quickly. So what did she think was going to happen next? That one day, he would just wake up and realize what he'd been missing?

In less than eight hours, she would be eighteen years old. Did she really want to kick off another year of her life sitting in a corner, waiting for Kane to notice her?

Hadn't she had enough?

"Okay," she said finally. "If you actually jump in that pool, then yes, I'll go out with you tonight."

With a holler, he jumped up and raced toward the pool. Miranda felt a warm tingling spread through her body at the thought that this guy was really going to go through with it, just to get a date with her. He stood on the edge and turned to face her, flashing her a peace sign.

"You won't be sorry!" he shouted, then spun around and, with an enormous splash, did a perfect belly flop into the deep end.

She was only sorry she'd hesitated.

The balcony was too high up for Kane to hear what was going on.

Still, he managed to get the general idea.

Bad enough that their conversation stretched on for more than an hour. Worse yet that, after the lame pool stunt, Miranda rushed to the edge holding a towel, then wrapped it around him, rubbing his back for warmth.

The final blow: Jackson ditched the towel and, still dripping, took Miranda's hand. She let him, and they walked off together.

Kane had tried to call her cell, hoping to whisper a warning in her ear, but she wasn't answering. Too engrossed, apparently, by Jackson's pathetic sideshow. How could she fall for his act? She was too sharp for that, too guarded. Maybe, Kane thought, she was just playing Jackson, waiting for the right moment to make her move.

But Kane was forced to admit it was unlikely. Miranda might have been sharp when it came to calculus homework or Trivial Pursuit, but when it came to guys, she was clueless. He knew that firsthand.

Kane tightened his grip on the balcony railing, choosing not to wonder why he cared, or why it sickened him to see that slimeball holding Miranda's hand. This wasn't jealousy, and it certainly wasn't self-sacrifice—he wasn't planning to risk his own standing with Jackson to protect Miranda from her own mistakes.

But he couldn't stop thinking about it. Kane, who had always believed his only responsibility was to have fun and his only obligation was to himself, felt responsible for the situation. Obligated to Miranda,

To *Miranda*, of all people.

She was a good friend. She was, on the whole, more

tolerable to be around than nearly anyone he knew. She let him get away with anything—though never without a sharp rebuke that cut deeper than she knew. And, clueless or not, she didn't deserve Jackson.

Staging a rescue attempt would be totally inconvenient—and, for all he knew, unwelcome. But it was also the right thing to do.

There was just one problem: Kane had wide variety of skills, talents, and areas of expertise.

Doing the right thing definitely wasn't one of them.

chapter

7

As soon as she stepped outside the club, Beth realized she had no idea how to get back to the hotel. They'd driven over in Star*la's car, and she didn't have enough cash on her for a taxi. Even if she could get a cab driver to take her to a bank and wait while she hit the ATM, there wouldn't be much point: Her tiny savings account was even emptier than usual. She'd drained it for gas and food money, figuring this trip would be worth it.

After all, now that she'd decided to take college off the table, what was the point in saving her money? What was she saving it *for*?

Emergencies, perhaps. Like this one.

A screeching crowd of girls burst out of the bar, slamming into Beth as they charged toward the street. She stumbled backward, catching herself just before she fell.

"Watch yourself!" a tall, skinny girl in knee-high leather boots yelled. "You're in the way!"

That part, she'd already figured out.

Maybe she could walk back. Beth knew this wasn't like home, where everything was within a couple miles of everything else. It could take all night—but she had nowhere else to be. Nor was she in any particular hurry to get back to the hotel room, because then she'd have to address the question: What next? Reed would have to return eventually. (Beth tried to ignore the persistent voice in her head pointing out that, no, Reed didn't *have* to come back— not if he got a better offer.)

Unable to decide and unwilling to turn back, she stood in front of the bar, watching the traffic crawl by.

She didn't hear his footsteps behind her, but she recognized his voice when he whispered her name. She still flinched when he put his arms around her and leaned his chin on her shoulder.

"What's going on?" Reed asked. His hair brushed against her neck. "Where'd you go?"

Beth didn't know how to answer. Now that she had to put it into words, her fears seemed ridiculous.

"I'm not feeling well," she lied.

"So you leave without saying good-bye?" He turned her around to face him. Their noses were almost touching. "How were you going to get back?"

Beth shrugged.

"What's really going on?"

She looked away. "Nothing."

He took her chin and tipped her face up so she couldn't avoid his dark eyes. "Tell me."

Beth took a deep breath. "When I saw you with *her*, I just thought—"

With both hands, Reed, smoothed down her hair, then

pressed her head against his chest. His T-shirt was so old and worn that the cotton felt like skin. "I'm sorry."

Her eyes widened. She'd been expecting denials, laughter, maybe even ridicule. Anything but a simple apology. Guys didn't work that way. "For what?"

"For making you think that anything could ever—"

"She's just so much more . . . like you," Beth said weakly, wondering why she was encouraging the idea. "She—she fits in. And I . . ."

"You fit," Reed assured her. "Here." He laced his arms around her waist and held tight.

"That's not what I mean," Beth protested.

"But that's what matters." When she didn't answer him, he ran a hand through his tangles of black curls. "Look. I know I don't . . ." He pressed his lips together and closed his eyes. When he opened them, she realized she could see her reflection. "All this—" He waved his arm at the club, the people, and, somewhere inside, Star*la. "You're right, it's me. And you're different. But that's why . . . You make *me* want to be different, you know? You make me think I can be better, that, like, I should be better. And . . ." He rubbed his hand against her back in a slow, soft circle. "You get that there's something else, something beside all this. I don't have to *be* anyone for you. All these people? They think they know, but they don't get it. They don't get *me*. You do."

It was the most he'd ever said to her at once. She tipped her head up to him, but before she could respond, he leaned down and kissed her. She closed her eyes, and the world beyond his lips disappeared.

"This is what I want," Reed told her. "You. Believe me?"

Beth realized she did. And always had. Reed was so

open about everything. He never did anything he didn't want to do, he never shaded the truth, and he never broke his word.

And that was the problem. Because Beth could never tell the real truth, and everything she said and did, every kiss, every smile was a lie. She didn't deserve to be with Reed, the one person in the world who had the most reason to hate her, but she was too weak to push him away. At the beginning, Beth had promised herself that she would end this before she got in too deep. But she'd let it go on, and now she couldn't imagine how she would make it through a day without Reed. He couldn't ever find out about her ever-present misery; but she couldn't survive it without him.

She was too much of a coward to let him go. But if he'd done it for her, she realized, that would have been it. An easy way out. If he had pushed her aside for Star*la, it would have destroyed her—but at least it would all be over, and she would no longer need to pretend to be happy or ignore the suffocating guilt.

She had *wanted* her suspicions to come true, wanted him to cheat on her. It would have been hard, but not as hard as telling the truth. This way—the Star*la way—she could have just slipped out the back and faded from his life. No messy scenes, no recriminations, no admissions. No pain.

"Beth?" he asked again when she didn't answer. "Do you believe me?"

She couldn't trust herself to speak, so she just nodded.

"Come back to the hotel with me," he suggested. "Let's forget this whole shitty day ever happened, and start over. Okay?"

I don't deserve you, she wanted to say. *I deserve to stay here, walking the streets, alone and miserable. I deserve to be alone forever.*

But she was weak. Too weak to confess her crime, too terrified to face her punishment. So she nodded again, and took his hand.

Kane had orchestrated his share of schemes, but he wasn't used to sneaking around to carry them out. He'd always preferred the bold lie to the snoop and spy—but in this case, it couldn't be helped. Miranda wasn't answering her cell, and if Jackson caught sight of him, the deal could be thrown into jeopardy. So Kane was reduced to stalking from afar.

The things I do for—He caught himself then, not having an easy word to fill in the blank. He could be out drinking, gambling, hooking up, living it up, and instead he was threading his way through a crowded street, always staying at least ten feet behind his prey, ducking behind corners and into alleys when it seemed they might be onto him. It was on the cusp of being humiliating, and Kane still wasn't quite sure why he was bothering. So he put the question out of his mind and focused on the chase.

They began the date at Sunset Terrace, a nauseatingly romantic bar overlooking the Strip. Miranda and Jackson placed their orders, then took their drinks out onto the wide outdoor deck, walking a little too closely together for Kane's comfort.

No matter. Kane knew just how to handle this— Jackson had made it easy on him.

He strode up to the bar, keeping a laserlike focus on the couple to make sure they didn't glance back inside, then beckoned the bartender toward him. "So, when did they pass the law?" he asked. "I would have thrown a party."

The bartender, a brawny guy in a light blue polo shirt and ill-fitting slacks, slung a towel over his shoulder and scowled at Kane. "What law?"

"The law lowering the drinking age." Kane gave him a serene, wide-eyed smile.

"What the hell are you talking about?"

Now Kane shrugged. The sneaking around part had been ignominious, but this was pure fun. "I just assumed," he said innocently. "After all, I know that girl over there"— he pointed at Miranda—"and she's only seventeen. But since you served her, anyway . . ." Kane had been watching closely enough to know that Miranda hadn't even had to flash her pathetic fake ID. "It's weird, though, since I probably would have heard about a new law like that, what with my dad being on the state liquor board and all."

Bingo.

"Shit." The bartender's jaw dropped, and he stepped out from behind the bar.

Kane winked at him. "Don't tell her I tipped you off, and no one has to know you're serving anyone old enough to walk."

"Deal," the bartender agreed. As he stalked off toward Beth and Jackson, Kane ducked out of the bar and positioned himself behind a large column just outside the entrance. He wished he could have stayed to watch the fall-out, but he had a rich imagination.

His hopes were confirmed a moment later, when the bartender appeared in the doorway, one hand wrapped tightly around Jackson's arm, the other firmly at Miranda's shoulder blades. "Nice try, kiddies," he growled, pushing them both onto the street. "Come back when she's potty-trained."

Kane was close enough to hear Miranda apologize—and close enough to see that Jackson wasn't about to give up that easily.

"No worries," he assured her, rubbing her shoulder in sympathy.

A weasel, Kane thought, but an effective one.

"If you want to go," Miranda began, "I totally—"

"*We're* going," Jackson told her. "And I know just the place."

They set off and, with a deep sigh, Kane followed. So the game wouldn't end as quickly as Kane would have liked, but it would still certainly end in his favor. Jackson didn't know who he was playing against.

In fact, to Kane's great benefit, Jackson didn't know he was playing at all. And that was Kane's favorite way to win.

"I can*not* believe you talked me into this," Harper groused as a line of Elvises spread out across the stage in a Rockettes-like kickline.

Adam clinked his glass against her Blue Hawaii daiquiri and took a sip from his All Shook Up vodka tonic. It was just as disgusting as it looked. "How can you not be enjoying this?" he asked, grinning widely. When Miranda had called to cancel that night's prebirthday dinner, it had taken Adam only twenty minutes of concentrated wheedling to convince Harper that the Elvis Extravaganza might be their best bet.

Not that Adam had nurtured any particular desire to

see a two-hour parade of Elvis impersonators, spanning the eras from *Ed Sullivan Show* chic to bloated 70s white jump-suits. But he also hadn't wanted the day to end.

They were the youngest people in the hall by more than a decade. But thanks to their new friend Margie, their free tickets placed them at a small table only a few feet from the stage. Adam could almost see his reflection in the fat Elvises' oversize sunglasses and gold medallion belts.

It was gaudy, tacky, and so noisy, he feared he'd be hear-ing "Jailhouse Rock" echo in his ears for weeks. But Harper wasn't arguing with him, attacking him, or running away from him, so Adam concluded it was worth it.

"Remind you of anything?" he asked suddenly. The so-called music was so loud that no one could hear them talking, even at normal volume—they could barely hear themselves. "Sixth grade?"

She looked puzzled for a second, then burst into laugh-ter. "Oh, my God, I can't believe you remember that."

Their teacher had been one of those naïve, overeager, twenty-two-year-olds who had yet to realize that Grace, CA, was about as dead as dead ends could get. Ms. Carpenter had quickly tired of the explorers, the Civil War, and the Great Depression, and had skipped forward to what she saw as the fundamental development of American history: the creation of rock-'n'-roll. They'd formed groups, and each had been charged with reenacting a per-formance of some famous group from the past. Complete with costumes and offbeat lip-synching.

"If you'd just listened to me in the first place," Harper said, giggling, "it never would have happened."

"If I'd listened to you in the first place, I would have

ended up wearing a dress." Harper had done her best to convince Adam to join up with her and Miranda . . . to perform as The Supremes. By the time Harper pulled out the spangly sequined miniskirts she had discovered in her parents' attic, Adam was out the door and halfway down the block.

He'd opted to go solo, and there was only one true option: Elvis Presley, the King. His rendition of "Jailhouse Rock" had brought the audience to its feet within seconds. (Not much of an accomplishment, considering the audience was made up entirely of sixth graders—half of whom already wanted to date him.) Harper had helped him tape black stripes to his white shirt for an excellent convict effect, and choreographed a dance for him. It all went perfectly . . . until he climbed up on his chair, kicked his leg out while strumming his air guitar—and slipped off the chair, flipping through the air and landing in a tangled, broken heap.

He'd hobbled around on crutches for the next two months, with a broken ankle almost as painful as his new nickname: the Klutz King.

"I still blame you," Adam said, waving an accusing finger in Harper's face. "If you hadn't suckered me into doing that stupid chair dance—"

"If *you* hadn't fallen on your ass—"

"I might never have become the man I am today," Adam concluded jokingly. He clapped Harper on the back. "I guess I owe it all to you."

Her grin faded suddenly, and she looked away, taking a long sip of the drink that looked even more disgusting than his. "Yeah."

"What's wrong?"

"Nothing." But she lowered her head, letting her wild wavy hair fall across her eyes. He knew it wasn't accidental. She was hiding.

"What is it, Gracie?" He hesitated, remembering that the last time he'd tried using his childhood nickname for her, she'd blasted him for his presumption that their history together still mattered. "What's wrong?" He used to be able to read her, and know why she was upset almost before she did. But this year, too much had happened—too much had changed. "Is it the tickets?" he guessed. "Miranda will never even know you were trying to get them for her. So she won't be disappointed. I'm sure we can think of something else great to surprise her with."

Harper laughed, but it was a sad sound. "I don't care about the stupid tickets," she admitted, her voice muffled. She was speaking so softly, he could barely hear her over the music, but what she said next was clear enough that he could almost read her lips. "It's . . . you. I miss you."

His first sensation: relief. Pure and overwhelming. Adam had to grip the edge of his chair to hold himself still. He didn't know what to say next. Their friendship—what was left of it—was so fragile, he feared that the wrong words could smash it beyond repair. "I—"

But before he could say anything, right or wrong, one of the white jumpsuit Elvises hopped off the stage and strolled right up to their table, close enough that Adam could see the plastic studs holding the rhinestones in place. "How about a serenade for our young lovers here?" the Elvis asked, and the audience roared with approval. Harper's face flushed red, and Adam wished he could hide under the table—or, better yet, shove the Elvis under there until he and Harper had safely left the building. But they did nothing, and Elvis began to sing.

"*Love me tender,*" he crooned. "*Love me true . . .*"

Adam buried his face in his hands, but it didn't make the nightmare end.

"*For my darlin' I love you. And I always will.*"

". . . and let's just say that I will never again bite into something without checking to see if it's still breathing," Jackson concluded, shaking his head as if in dismay at his own foolishness.

Miranda laughed—perhaps a little harder than the story merited, but then, she was spending her birthday with a cute, older guy who, in his own words, thought she was "adorable," "hilarious," and "fantastic." A little extra laughter was a small price to pay. "That's unbelievable," she said, gasping for breath.

"I swear." Jackson put a hand over his heart. "It happened exactly like I said."

When they'd been booted out of the bar, Miranda had been sure her date was over before it even began, but Jackson had just shrugged and escorted her down the strip to Killian's, a dark, opulent, outrageously Irish pub with thick burgers, heaping plates of mashed potatoes, and towering mugs of beer. Miranda stuck to salad and soda.

"I'm really glad you agreed to come out with me tonight," Jackson told her.

Miranda searched for a suitably snappy response, but under the table she suddenly felt the light touch of a hand on her knee, and her witty bravado melted away. "Me too," she said sincerely, and, though it felt unthinkably bold, she rested her hand on top of his, lightly twining their fingers. Jackson stared at her so intensely that she was tempted to look away, but she knew that in a situation like this, she was supposed to meet his eyes. So she forced herself to do it.

He's gazing *at me,* the overanalytical part of her mind that refused to shut up observed. *I never thought anyone would do that.* It was only a few hours to her birthday, and Miranda allowed herself to hope that she would get to start off her eighteenth year in the best way imaginable: with a kiss.

"Can I get you anything else?" the waitress asked, appearing as if from nowhere. She was dressed in green from head to toe, and wore a four-leaf clover beret over her bright red—certainly dyed—hair. "Some more water?"

"We're fine," Jackson said, but she had already leaned in to start pouring.

"Jesus!" he screeched, as half a pitcher of ice water sloshed into his lap. He jumped up, but it was too late—a large dark spot was quickly spreading across the front of his pants.

"Oh, I'm so sorry!" the waitress cried, slipping out of the fake Irish brogue she'd adopted for the rest of their meal. "Here, let me—" She leaned toward him to start patting him down with a napkin, but Jackson squirmed away. "I got it," he snapped. Sliding out of the booth. "Miranda, I've got to—"

"Go," she urged him, marveling at how quickly her perfect date could go south. Not that it was a surprise. The perfection of the afternoon had seemed bizarre. It was all too unbelievably smooth and perfect to be true. This comedy of errors, on the other hand, was totally in keeping with the way Miranda's life usually went. "I think the bathroom's that way." She pointed, but he was already gone. *He'll come back in a minute,* she assured herself, but she couldn't make herself believe it.

"Clumsy waitress, eh?" a familiar voice chuckled from the next booth over. Miranda peeked her head over the top of her booth to see Kane staring up at her. He shook his head. "It's so hard to find good help these days."

As always, she felt an unmitigated blast of joy at seeing him—so it took her a moment to wonder at his presence. "What are you doing here?" she finally asked.

"You're not answering your phone," he pointed out.

"I'm on a *date.*"

He smirked. "Yeah. I caught that. How's it going?"

"It's going great," she boasted. "Fantastically. Best date I ever had." Mostly because all her other dates had sucked. But that wasn't the point. The point was to let Kane know that he wasn't welcome to crash this one.

Even if, secretly, possibly, he was.

"I was afraid of that."

"Afraid of what? That I'd actually have a good time?" Dare she allow herself to hope that he was jealous? *Stop,* she instructed herself. *It doesn't matter. I'm here with Jackson.* Jackson was cute, smart, sweet, and, though he wasn't Kane, he had one important thing going for him that Kane didn't: He wanted to be with Miranda.

"He's bad news," Kane told her. "Don't trust him. I'd leave now, if I were you, now that I've given you the chance."

"Now that you've . . . ?" The pieces fell into place: the

suddenly clumsy waitress. The fact that Kane just *happened* to be sitting at the next table. Maybe even the bartender who'd randomly thrown them out of the bar. "Are you trying to ruin my life? Or just my night?"

"Just trying to help," Kane said. "Get away from him. He's—uh-oh. Don't tell him I was here." Before she could say anything else, Kane had ducked out of the booth and disappeared into a corridor. And then Jackson was back.

"Well, I've gone from soggy to damp," Jackson said ruefully, sliding back into his seat. "So that's an improvement. Still, maybe after dinner we could stop by my room, just to grab a change of clothes. If you're up for it, I mean."

It didn't make any sense. This was Kane's friend; Kane was the one who'd introduced them. He'd vouched for Jackson. And now he was trying to torpedo the date? It was as if he was jealous, but he *couldn't* be jealous. And it didn't matter either way. It didn't matter what his reasoning was. She'd wasted enough of her time worrying about Kane—this was her chance to actually be happy, even if it was just for the night. She wasn't going to screw it up. "Sure, as soon as we're done here, we should definitely hit your room so you can get out of those wet pants." She giggled as they both realized the implications of what she'd just said. They weren't altogether unintentional.

Miranda was about to continue, to tell Jackson about the strange encounter she'd had while he was drying off, so that they could laugh about and then dismiss Kane's ludicrous scheming. But Kane had asked her not to say anything.

And though she didn't owe him anything, didn't care what he wanted, and refused to spend another moment thinking about him, she kept her mouth shut.

Her skin was so soft.

Everything about her was perfect. That sweet, lilting voice that sang whenever she spoke. Her hair, which fell through his fingers like it had no substance, no weight, but was made of golden light. Her lips, which were now pressed against his neck, and her fingers, which crawled down his bare chest and massaged his back. Her pale blue eyes, closed now, shaded by delicate eyelids rimmed by eyelashes so light, they were nearly invisible.

But it was her skin that Reed loved the most. The cheap hotel sheets were scratchy, but her pale, creamy skin was unbelievably soft and smooth, as if it had never been exposed to the outside world. Reed loved the way it felt against his cheek, his lips, his fingertips, his body—always wondering how something that delicately perfect could exist. And how it could be within his grasp.

She moaned softly, and shivered as he traced his fingers lightly down the small of her back. He grabbed her waist, gently tipping her onto her back and rolling on top of her, so their chests breathed together and their lips met. He supported his weight on his elbows, so as not to crush her, and stared down at her.

Whatever doubts he'd had at the beginning, whatever guilt he'd struggled with, he was past that now. He had no regrets.

"Do you . . . do you want to?" she whispered suddenly, her eyes still closed.

"Want to what?" He kissed her cheek, then her forehead, her nose, and, finally, her lips.

"You know." She opened her eyes. A tear was pooling

in one of the corners. "I don't know if you brought . . . protection." It sounded like she had to choke the word out. "But if you did, maybe we should—"

Reed rolled off of her and propped himself up on his side. "Where's this coming from?"

Beth tucked a strand of hair behind her ear and, instead of turning to face him, stayed on her back, staring up at the cracked ceiling. "I know I said I didn't want to, not yet, but that was before . . ."

"Before what?" When she didn't answer, he sat up, and pulled her up too. "Before *what*?"

"You're just really good to me, and I thought—" She took his hand in hers. "I want to make you happy."

"You think *this* will make me happy?" he asked incredulously, his voice rising. "You're doing this as if—as if you owe me something? Do you think I'm that kind of guy? That I'd ever want you to—"

"Are you mad?" Her voice sounded like a child's.

"Of course not!" He forced himself to stop and take a few deep breaths. "I just don't get it. Why would you think . . . I told you I'd wait. I told you I didn't care."

"I know. But . . ."

She didn't need to say it out loud. He got it: She hadn't believed him.

Reed didn't know much about Beth's past, so he didn't know who had screwed her over so badly, or how. But something must have happened to make her so unwilling to trust that someone would wait for her.

"Why now?" he asked. "Why tonight?"

"Because I don't deserve you," she admitted. "And I just thought maybe . . . I don't know." She threw herself back down on the bed, face first, her head buried in her arms. "I don't get why you want . . . I don't know why anyone would want to be with me," she mumbled, her voice muffled by the sheets. Her body trembled, and Reed wondered if she was crying.

It didn't make sense. He was the stoner. The dumbass. The loser. She was smart, beautiful, perfect. Grace's princess. He was the one who didn't belong in the picture, who was undeserving. How could someone so smart miss something so obvious?

"Come on," he said. She didn't sit up, just shook her head, still hiding her face as if afraid to show him her tears. "Come on," he repeated. "For me."

Finally, she lifted her head, wiping clumsily at her tears like a little kid. Her makeup smeared across her face. "Where?"

"You'll see."

He took her by the hand and led her out of the room, down the hall to the elevators and, when they'd stepped inside, pressed the button for the top floor. Moments later they stepped out onto an identical hallway, and Reed, once again leading the way, guided Beth down to the opposite end and through a half-hidden door.

"I did a little exploring," Reed explained as they entered the dark, cramped stairwell, though she hadn't asked, or even spoken since they'd left the room. "Found something I thought you'd like." They climbed up two flights of stairs, pushed through a heavy door at the top, and found themselves standing on the roof, surrounded by the tall silhouettes of the Camelot's fake turrets. "Come on," he urged Beth, leading her toward the edge. She followed as if she'd lost all momentum of her own—as if, were he to let go, she would stand motionless until given another command.

They stood at the rim of the roof, the lights of Vegas spread out beneath them like stolen gems spilled onto a sheet of black velvet. A small smile crept onto Beth's face, still streaked with mascara-stained tears.

"Remember that first day, on the crater?" Reed asked. She nodded. They had hiked up to the top and, surrounded by miles of empty desert wilderness, had decided to take a chance. Together. Reed realized he was breathing quickly and tried to calm himself down. He'd been steeling himself to do this at some point in the weekend—but now that he was actually here, and the words he'd never said before were ready to come out, he could barely speak. "Beth, since then, being with you—it's not what I expected. It's—" He hadn't rehearsed; that would have been lame. But now that he was here, he almost wished he'd prepared something to say. When he wrote a song, the words always came pouring out. But actually *talking* about the way he felt—especially to someone else—was different. It was almost impossible.

He had to try.

"I used to think it was just something people said, you know? Some obligation, but it didn't mean anything." He knew he wasn't making much sense, but it was a place to start, and she was listening. "I didn't care. And when I met you, I didn't care about anything. And then . . ." He put his arms around her shoulders, resting his hands loosely at the nape of her neck. "Now. It's different. You know?"

"I don't . . . I don't get what you're trying to say," Beth said slowly, her face pale. "Are you breaking up with me?"

"No. No!" This was going all wrong. Reed wished he'd had a joint ahead of time, because then he wouldn't care so much and it wouldn't matter if it came out wrong. But then, it wouldn't have mattered at all—that's how it had always been, before her.

Sober was hard, but if he was going to do this—do this and *mean* it—it was necessary.

"I'm trying to tell you—" He couldn't look at her while he was saying it, so he turned to face the endless spread of lights, grasping her hand as he waited for the words to come. "I think . . . I love you."

Silence.

"Beth. I love you." It was easier this time. There was no more doubt.

But she didn't say anything. Finally, he dared to look at her—and she seemed so terrified, so appalled, that he quickly looked away.

"You can't," she whispered. "Take it back."

But Reed couldn't. "I love you," he said again.

She touched his cheek, gently, with that impossibly soft skin. "Reed . . ." He waited for her to say it back, to say *anything*. But instead, she let out a loud, anguished sob—and bolted.

"Beth!"

But she didn't hesitate, or look back. She raced across the roof, flung the door open and, just like that, she was gone.

chapter
8

Even after they'd stepped outside the building and into the relatively quiet night, Harper imagined she could still hear the oversynthesized chords of the love song echoing in her ears. It made the awkward silence a little easier to take.

"So," Adam finally said.

"So."

About a foot of distance lay between them, which seemed safest. Adam leaned against the wall of the hotel, the flashing Elvis billboard casting a series of red and gold lights across his face. He watched her as if expecting something.

She knew she was supposed to start. After all, she'd been the one to push him away. It was just that now she couldn't quite remember why.

He raised an arm and leaned it against the wall, his biceps bulging with even the small movement. And Harper imagined what it would feel like to have those biceps encircling her; to have free range to stroke his arms and lean against his chest and—

So that, obviously, was problem number one. Could she handle having him in her life without having *all* of him? It had been hard enough before, when all she'd had was her imagination. Now she had memories, and they were more insistent. They were more real.

But it had never been about that, or only that. It had been about Adam, the only person she could truly count on, the one who knew every detail of her past and was present in every dream of her future. She'd been miserable these last few months, and now that pain seemed pointless, the time wasted.

"You miss me," Adam prompted, when it became obvious that she wasn't going to begin.

Harper attempted a blasé expression. "You can be useful," she told him. "Occasionally."

Adam took a step toward her. "So, does that mean we can end this thing?" he asked casually.

Harper shrugged. "I guess."

"And you and me . . ."

"Yeah." Harper allowed herself a smile. "We're okay." That was the great thing about being friends with guys: They didn't need any of that sappy "I'm so sorry," "No, *I'm* so sorry" crap. They could just shrug and move on. Move forward.

Now Harper took a step, and they met in the middle. She wanted to wait for Adam to move first, but her patience ran short, and she threw her arms around his waist, pressing her head against his chest, feeling like she had come home. Adam wrapped her into a tight bear hug, his cheek pressed against the top of her head.

"I really did miss you," she murmured, thinking it would be too soft for him to hear.

"I know," he whispered back. Then, louder, in a more teasing voice, "You know you can't live without me."

No, she couldn't.

When they finally broke from the hug, he didn't release her, just loosened his arms enough that she could lean away from his body and look up at him. The Vegas night was lit by enough neon to see every chiseled feature of his face in sharp relief, from his squarish, dimpled chin to his regal brow line and deep-set eyes. But Harper barely noticed any of that; he wasn't an assemblage of perfect pieces. He was just her best friend. "Adam, I—"

He kissed her.

Not on the forehead, not on the cheek. On the lips.

And not slowly, not gently, but hard, desperate, hungry. She closed her eyes and sucked his lower lip, nearly gasping as his tongue crept past her teeth and met hers, his breathing sped up, hers nearly stopped, and she drank him in. He tasted the same.

And then it was over, and just as roughly as he'd grabbed her, he pushed her away.

"What was—?" Harper, still stunned—and already missing his touch—tried to catch her breath.

"I don't know. I don't know." Adam was panting, leaning his fists against the wall. "I'm sorry, I don't—"

"You said you didn't want that. This," Harper reminded him. "You said friends." He couldn't trust her enough for a relationship, he'd told her. Things would get too messy, and they would lose each other again.

"I know what I said!" he snapped. Then he pressed a hand to his forehead. "I'm sorry. I don't . . . you were there, and it just felt . . ."

"Yeah." She wanted to touch him, but—she didn't want to touch him, not if it meant scaring him away. "We can just . . . forget it. If you want." *No, no, no,* she pleaded silently. *Say no.*

"Maybe. But . . ."

"But?" She tried to keep the tinge of hope out of her voice.

Harper leaned against the wall next to him, their faces once again only inches apart.

"If we did this—I mean, if we were going to do this, we'd have to decide," Adam said. "You know? It can't be . . ."

"Casual."

He took her hand, then dropped it a moment later and shoved his hands in his pockets. "I missed you too, Gracie. And I—I *miss* you. But when we were together, like that, it just . . ."

"I know."

"Everything got so fucked up."

Because of me, Harper thought. Adam was kind enough not to say it; but she knew he was thinking it too. He had to be. "Maybe we should just . . . forget it. Or, take some time."

"Yeah." He nodded to himself. "Maybe. That would be good. But . . ." He took her hand again, and this time, he pressed it to his chest, then tugged her toward him. Their lips nearly met when, with all the strength she could muster, Harper pushed him away. It nearly wasn't enough.

"No," she said firmly. "You should go."

"This could be the right thing," Adam told her. "Maybe I was wrong before, and this—maybe it could work."

She wanted to stay—she wanted to kiss him again, to make him remember what he was missing and convince him that he needed it as much as she did. But if he wasn't sure yet, then she couldn't risk it. If she let him back in and he changed his mind again—it would be too hard. For both of them.

Restraint wasn't in Harper's repertoire. But she could try. "You need to know," she told him. "You need to be sure."

"What if I told you I was sure?"

"Then you'd be lying."

He let out a pained laugh. "I hate that you know me like this."

"You love it."

"Yeah." He reached over and twisted his finger through her hair. "What time is it?"

She checked her cell. "Almost nine." Strange, it seemed later.

"Okay. You think. I'll think. And we'll meet later—"

"At midnight," Harper suggested. "But before you go, there's something . . . you need to know. . . ." She wanted to tell him her secret—to tell him the truth about Kaia, and the accident. He deserved to know who she really was, and he deserved the chance to push her away.

And maybe . . . he deserved the chance to forgive.

"What?" he asked, after a long pause.

But she couldn't do it. She would, she promised herself, but only when she knew what was at stake. If he decided that he needed her as much as she needed him, then she would know she could trust him to keep her secret. Maybe she could even trust him not to leave her. But it was too soon—he was still unsure of what he wanted. So she couldn't take the risk. "Nothing," she said quickly. "Save it for midnight."

"Where?"

Harper scanned the skyline, and her gaze stumbled over the towering replica of the Empire State Building. It reminded her of some movie—some lame romantic comedy, probably, but certainly one with a happy ending. And she could use that kind of luck. She pointed. "Up there, on the roof. Whatever you decide."

"I'll be there," he promised. "And Harper . . ." He gripped her shoulders. "Whatever happens next, we need to make it work. Because this friendship—you . . ."

"I know," she assured him. "You don't have to say it."

"Yes, I do." He hugged her again, his strong arms locking her into the embrace. "This friendship is everything, Gracie. I'm not losing you again."

Miranda finished the meal still hungry, so she allowed Jackson to talk her into dessert: a massive ice-cream sundae with three scoops of chocolate chip ice cream, a hearty helping of chocolate hazelnut sauce topped by two cherries, all piled atop a freshly baked double fudge brownie. Miranda had promised herself she would only have a couple bites—but it was already half gone.

"This is amazing," she moaned as another gulp of icy sweetness slid down her throat. And she wasn't just talking about the food. Kane's bizarre interruptions aside, the night had gone remarkably well. It was the kind of date other people had: normal, pleasant, engrossing and, hopefully, all leading up to a good night kiss. Or more.

This wasn't the way Miranda's life usually went, but it

was, after all, almost her birthday. Maybe the universe was giving her a present.

"*You're* amazing," Jackson told her, and scooped his spoon into the heaping sundae, then brought it to her ips. She sucked down another mouthful and, smiling at him, licked her lips. When Harper did that kind of thing, she always made it look incredibly sexy. Miranda suspected she just looked like a messy eater—but then, that's what she was, so it couldn't be helped. "Uh, you've still got a little on your face. . . ."

"Where?" Miranda asked, turning red. She slid her napkin across her lips and looked up at him. "Better?"

Jackson laughed. "Not really. There's still a little, just above your lips—no, not there—no, to the left . . . here." He leaned across the table and gave her such a soft, brief kiss that she could almost believe she'd imagined it. "Mmmm," he said, licking his own lips with a satisfied grin. "Sweet."

Miranda didn't know what to do. She brushed her fingers against her lips, as if to check that the smear of ice cream was really gone—or to find some trace evidence of his kiss. Her fingertips tingled.

They stared at each other, Miranda blushing and Jackson playing with the peace sign that hung on a chain around his neck. "You wanna get out of here?" Jackson finally said. "We could . . . go somewhere."

From the burning sensation in her cheeks, Miranda guessed that they had just turned from pale pink to fire engine red. But Jackson didn't seem to care. "I guess," she told him. "I'd like that."

Jackson gestured to the waitress that she should bring

over the bill, but when she returned, she wasn't alone. "This gentleman would like to speak with you," she said, stepping aside to make way for a short, squat guy in a security guard uniform. He pointed at Jackson's backpack.

"Open the bag for me, sir."

Jackson stood up, but made no motion toward his backpack. "What's this about?"

"I said, open the bag, *sir*. Or I'll open it for you."

"You can't just come here and—"

The security guy lunged for the bag and ripped it open before Jackson could stop him. He plunged his hand inside and pulled out a stack of candy bars and several plastic bags filled with green flakes. It looked like oregano. But Miranda knew it wasn't.

Jackson did a 180, dropping the offended bravado and starting to whine. "Look, man, give me a break, it's just my private stash, and I'm just trying to have a good time here—"

The security guard shook his head and waved the baggie in his face. "I don't think so, kid. You got a lot of shit in here. This looks like intent to distribute, to me. And you know what that means."

Miranda sat dumbstruck as the long arm of the law—or, in this case, the short, hairy arm—reached out, grabbed her date, and dragged him out of the restaurant, backpack and all. "Babe, I'm sorry!" Jackson cried as they hustled him away. "I'll call you. . . ."

In a moment he was gone, and she was left alone at an empty table, waiting for the check—which she would now have to cover herself. The whole restaurant was staring at her like she'd just turned green and sprouted antennae.

"Happy birthday to me," she muttered.

"It's not midnight yet," a voice pointed out. "There's still time for things to pick up."

"Did you do this?" she asked as Kane slid into the seat across from her, an even smugger than usual grin painted across his face. "Are you fucking kidding me? *Did you do this?*"

She'd never been so angry with him—she'd never been angry at him at all, in fact, since usually his careless smirk and halfhearted apologies charmed the emotion out of her before it had a chance to take root. But charm could only go so far.

"It was for your own good, Stevens."

"Oh, really?" The sarcasm felt good, like she was in control again. And when he flinched at the cool anger in her voice, that was even better. "And how exactly do you figure that?"

"He was a dealer, Stevens."

"So you got him arrested?" It's not that Miranda wanted to date a drug dealer—and, she had to admit, there was a ring of truth in Kane's words, especially given what she'd just seen of his supply—but still, he hadn't seemed like a bad guy. And he'd kissed her.

"The security guard's a friend of mine," Kane explained. "He'll take him outside, give him a good scare, confiscate his stash, then let him go. Don't worry about him—he's not worth your time."

"What do you know?" she retorted.

"I know he has a girlfriend."

"You're lying."

"No."

It was like getting punched in the stomach. "Oh." She

sank back in her seat, stared up at the ceiling, and wondered how she could have been so stupid.

"I didn't know," Kane said. "Not at first, and then—it was too late."

"Uh-huh." She'd been so excited, imagining that a cute college guy might actually be interested. And what did he turn out to be? A drug dealer with a girlfriend. Killing time. "So, what? He was just using me or something?" Why even bother, Miranda wondered. It's not like she was hot—it's not like this city wasn't filled with beautiful women. Why pick on Miranda, unless he just got some sadistic joy out of stringing her along and watching her get her pathetic little hopes up? "So this was all some kind of game?" she guessed bitterly, trying to make her lower lip stop trembling. She didn't want Kane to know how close she was to tears. "Get the pathetic loser to fall for him, go back to his room, and then—?"

"No, that's not it," Kane said quickly. He slid across to the other side of the booth and put an arm around her. "He really liked you. He did." But she could hear the lie in his words. "He wasn't good enough for you, Stevens."

"I guess no one is," Miranda spit out. "Maybe *that's* my problem. That's why I'm always ending up alone. I'm just too fabulous, right?" She closed her eyes and pressed a hand across her face, hoping he wouldn't notice her sniffling. "I'm not going to thank you, you know," she informed him, trying to sound strong.

"Wouldn't expect you to."

"You don't need to pull asinine stunts like that just to rescue me from my own idiocy. I'm a big girl."

"The biggest. Elephantine."

A giggle sputtered out through her tears. "Shut up."

"I often say to myself, "That Miranda, she is truly an Amazonian giant among men. Doesn't need any help from anyone, and too big to fit inside normal-size buildings. It's—'"

"*Shut up,*" she repeated, laughing and elbowing him in the side.

"That's better." He gave her a soft shove back. "So what now?"

Miranda tried to gather herself together. She took a deep breath. "I guess I should call Harper and tell her the date . . . ended early. She'll probably want to hang out." She reached for her cell phone, but he caught her wrist.

"What's your hurry?"

"You have a better idea?" she asked. He hadn't yet let go of her wrist.

"Always. We get out of here, and I make things up to you." He raised an eyebrow. "Think you'll be able to forgive me?"

"Maybe," she allowed. "If you behave."

The charming smile returned with a vengeance. "Not a chance."

She didn't know what she was doing or where she was going, she just knew that she had to get away. He couldn't be in love with her. He *couldn't.*

Beth burst through the doors of the hotel and huddled under the front awning, shaking, barely aware of the tears streaming down her face. She curled her hands into fists, digging her nails into her palms, as if the pain would make things clearer. It didn't.

He was in love with her.

She had killed his girlfriend.

He was in love with her.

She was a murderer.

As soon as the words were out of his mouth, Beth had known that her time was up. She had to confess everything. But it was too hard.

She hated herself for her weakness, and for her terror. Was she in love with him too?

She didn't allow herself to wonder.

A tall, too-skinny guy wandered up to her and, though she couldn't face anyone, she didn't have the will to turn away. "No one that pretty should be that sad," he told her.

Beth took a closer look at his familiar face. It was the guy she'd seen earlier, with Kane. As if the night wasn't bad enough. "Are you staying here?" *Or just following me?*

"Looking for someone," the guy muttered. "But she's not here. Lucky I found you."

"Can you just leave me alone?" Beth wasn't even sure she meant it. At least talking to him was helping to drive Reed's words out of her mind. *I love you.* How could she believe that when she hated herself so much? Who could ever love her, once they knew what she really was?

"Whatever. But first." He reached into his pocked and pulled out a lumpy, misshapen joint. "Pigs got everything else, but this one's special. Guaranteed to brighten your night. My treat."

Common sense would tell her not to accept drugs from strangers—especially strangers who associated with Kane. But common sense had gone to sleep for the night, and Beth needed something to get her through the next

ROBIN WASSERMAN

minute, and the one after that. She reached for the joint.
The guy handed it to her, then, as she turned to go, he
grabbed her other hand, squeezing tight. "Not so fast. I'm
not done with you."

Whatever he was about to do, she deserved worse. So
she didn't pull back, didn't scream, didn't show a hint of
fear. She wasn't feeling any. She felt dead inside, flat and
hopeless. Her mind flashed a danger sign, but her body and
her emotions refused to react. Whatever happened, would
happen.

The guy reached into his pocket again, and Beth saw a
glint of metal.

He pulled out a lighter, stuck the joint between her
lips, and lit the tip. "Enjoy the night," he said, already walking away. "Someone should."

She drew in deep, gulping down the bitter smoke. And
again. A burning cloud filled her lungs, searing her insides,
and it almost made her smile. Because she knew that soon
the cloudy haze would descend and she wouldn't have to
worry about anything anymore, not for a long while.

Her muscles went loose as her senses intensified, and
the world seemed to get stronger and brighter with every
breath. The joint burned out, but the lights and colors
around her continued to brighten, until the world seemed
to pulse with a rippling energy that drew the earth and sky
together into a living creature poised to consume her.

This was new. And it felt wrong.

Beth turned to look for Kane's friend, but he was gone,
disappeared into the crowd, and as she turned in a slow circle searching for him, she found she couldn't stop, and her
spinning grew faster and faster until she was whirling

wildly, her hands outstretched and her face tipped up to the sky. She stumbled as the ground tilted toward her, then rolled away, and as she flung her arms out for balance, she saw an impossible trail of blue tracing through the air following her movements. Suddenly the colors were everywhere, bursting out of people's heads like a Crayola explosion, wiggling and swirling through the air until mixing into a thick, heavy, mud-colored fog that pressed down upon her until she fell to the ground under its weight.

She pressed herself against the wall, crawling, almost slithering, around the corner, out of sight, hiding from whatever was out there, watching, waiting. And in the darkness of the alley, she curled into a tight ball, pressing her legs against her chest and digging her chin into them, trying to think. But her thoughts kept bobbing to the surface and dipping below again, just before she could pluck them away . . . they were too fast, she was too slow.

This isn't pot.

He loves me.

I killed her.

What if they find me?

What is this?

What's happening to me?

What will happen to me?

Help . . .

That was the right thought, the important one, the one she should turn into words and scream aloud before she got dragged under, but it was so hard to focus, and before she could speak, the idea drifted away.

So did she.

145

chapter

9

It was all clear to him now.

Standing so close to Harper, breathing in her perfume, it had been too hard to think rationally. But a couple hours of wandering the streets had given Adam everything he needed to be certain.

It was a frightening choice. Sticking to friendship would be the safe move, that much was obvious. But what if Harper was supposed to be the one?

Not that Adam believed in that cheesy shit. That was for girls, long-distance commercials, and Valentine's Day. Still, he couldn't forget how happy he'd been for those few weeks they were together, and how right it had felt to hold her again.

But on the other hand—and it seemed there was always another hand—coming together had nearly blown them apart for good. He had meant what he'd told her in the hospital, months before: He loved her, he forgave her, but he wasn't ready to trust her. He couldn't force himself to forget the lies she'd told and the pain she'd caused. She'd manipulated him and destroyed his relationship with Beth, all to get what she wanted.

And, despite how easy it was to believe otherwise when looking into her eyes, he suspected she'd be willing to do it all over again.

Within minutes of leaving her side, he'd known exactly what to do. An hour later, he'd changed his mind, just as sure that he was right. Eventually, he'd gone back to the hotel room—half hoping to run into Kane or Miranda, *someone* he could ask for advice, even though he knew that no one could help. Not with this. The room had been empty, and he lay down on the bed, closed his eyes, and tried to decide what he wanted.

Was it more important to be happy? Or to protect himself from being miserable?

It was almost midnight, and he finally knew the answer. He just didn't know what Harper would do when she heard it.

He had intended to walk to their rendezvous point— the New York-New York hotel, with its neon and plaster skyline, was less than a mile away. But now it was too late for that. So instead he was forced to wait in front of the hotel for the taxi, shifting his weight back and forth, nervously wondering how the night would end.

If he hadn't been looking for something, anything, to take his mind off of things, he might never have heard the noise, a soft, muffled whimpering, like an injured animal. He almost certainly wouldn't have gone in search of its source. And so he would never have discovered the girl huddled in the alley, dirty blond hair spilling in a thick curtain around her face, her hands wrapped around her knees. She was rocking back and forth, muttering the same phrase over and over again, until the words blended together into a string of nonsense syllables.

"I did it. I did it. I didit. I didit. IdiditIdiditIdidit . . ."

He should have recognized the voice, or the hair, or the way her fingers trembled as they clasped her lower legs and pulled them tighter to her chest. But it wasn't until he put a hand on her shoulder, leaned down, and asked if she was all right that the girl tilted her head up, just a bit, but just enough, for him to understand.

"Oh, my God." Adam staggered backward with the shock. "Beth? What happened? Are you . . . okay?" He was almost afraid to hear the answer to the first question. The answer to the second was pointlessly obvious.

"Reed?" she whispered.

"It's Adam." The kernel of terror within him began to blossom.

She stared up at him and squinted as if she didn't recognize him. "What's going on? What are you what am I you need to go. I did it I did it I did it . . ."

Her pupils were overdilated, and her whole body was shaking. "Hey. Shhh, calm down." He put his arms around her and tried to help her stand up. "It's going to be okay." But was it? "Come on, let's get you up."

She resisted at first, curling tighter into herself, her muscles straining against his touch. Then, suddenly, all the tension flooded out of her, and she sagged in his arms. He stood, and she leaned against him, still conscious but no longer trembling. Her face was streaked with tears. "Is this what it was like for her?" she asked him plaintively, tugging at his collar. "Oh, God, did I do this to her? How could I do this?"

"I don't understand," Adam said gently, but she didn't seem to hear him.

"I did it. I deserve it. Ohgodohgodohgodohgod—" Her voice broke off into a heaving sob, and she buried her head in his shoulder. He stroked her hair and tried not to panic. Should he call 911? Should he find a doctor, get her to a hospital? Or just inside and up to the room? She didn't seem hurt, but—something was obviously wrong. Seriously wrong.

Upstairs, he decided. Calm her down, figure out what's happening, and then deal with it.

"It's okay, I'm here," he whispered, stroking her hair and trying to calm her sobs. He guided her into the lobby and toward the elevator bank, not even noticing the crowd's curious stares. He didn't have the mental space to worry about anything now except for Beth, and making sure she was okay.

"Where are we going?" she whispered. "Where are you taking me?"

"Somewhere safe," he promised. The room was still empty. He led her inside and sat her down on the bed. She didn't curl up again, or lie down. She just sat where he'd placed her, still clinging to him. He sat down beside her and gathered her in his arms.

"Don't hate me," she begged. "Not you, too. Please."

"Of course not." He kissed the top of her head. "I could never hate you."

"Don't leave me."

"I won't."

"I'm sorry for before," she said. "I shouldn't have let you say it. I should never have let you. And then I left. You should have left me."

"Don't worry." Adam wasn't even sure she knew who he was, much less what she was saying. "Don't apologize."

"But *I'm sorry!*" she wailed.

"I forgive you. I do. For everything."

"I love you, too," she said, throwing her arms around his neck and laying her head against his chest. "I should have said it. I love you, too."

He didn't know what to do, so he held her until she stopped crying. And when she did, he still held her, and listened intently to her shallow but even breaths, wishing that he could save her from whatever was tearing her apart.

He didn't notice the time passing, and when his cell phone rang, again and again, he barely heard it. His world had narrowed to a single point, and a single mission: protecting Beth.

She needed him. And for now, that was all that mattered.

It wasn't like him to be late.

The balcony atop the fake Empire State Building was nearly empty this time of night, and Harper leaned against the railing looking out over the lights, wondering.

She dialed his number again, but he still didn't pick up.

Maybe something happened to him, she thought. But she knew nothing had. He had obviously made his decision, and couldn't even be bothered to tell her to her face. *Maybe there's still a chance,* she told herself. *It's possible.*

But he was almost an hour late. This was Vegas, a town full of dreamers hoping that their big win would come through despite million-to-one odds. They stayed at the table hour after hour, night after night, waiting for their luck to turn.

Harper was a realist; she knew when to fold.

She just couldn't bring herself to leave—because giving up would mean admitting that Adam didn't want her, that he didn't even think enough of her to explain why. So much for the friendship he refused to lose; so much for the two of them being all that mattered.

The city twinkled below her, and Harper wondered what the view might be like from the real Empire State Building, so much taller than this lame cardboard copy. She'd only seen it in movies, but Kaia, who never tired of reminiscing about her hometown, had once tried to describe it. "You can imagine you're standing at the edge of the world," she had said. By day, you would see Central Park in one direction—and here, thanks to Kaia's descriptions, Harper always imagined an overgrown jungle brimming with out-of-work artists, horny couples, and needle junkies. From the other end, Kaia claimed, you could see across the whole island of Manhattan, down to its narrow tip and beyond. "You can even see *Brooklyn,*" Kaia had said in a hushed voice, as if Brooklyn were an exotic foreign land of hidden wonders.

But the view during the day was nothing compared with the view at night, when the city lit up and you could chart the lives of a million people by the flickering and streaming of an infinity of lights.

Standing here in the dark, bracing against the wind and watching the neon flash and shimmer, it was easy to imagine she was thousands of miles away, somewhere *real.* She thought that if she tried hard enough, she could probably convince herself that Kaia was standing next to her in the darkness.

But Harper was still a realist—and Kaia was still dead.

"He's not coming," she said aloud, testing out the sound of the words. She knew she should leave and get on with her night—but that would mean getting on with her *life*. Without Adam. And she wasn't ready for that.

"He's not coming," she said again, louder.

There was no one there to hear her, and no one to know that she decided not to leave. Not yet. Long ago, Adam had asked her to trust him, and to trust their friendship. She would wait, just a little longer.

Maybe she was wrong, and he hadn't abandoned her.

Maybe he was coming after all. So she held on to the railing, looked out at the landscape that glittered like a desert sky, and waited.

If he cared about her at all, he would come.

The world faded in.

Bright seeped into shadow, light searing her eyes and then disappearing into a dark cloud. She felt like she was flying. She felt like she was sailing. She felt like she was drowning.

She felt still and safe, wrapped in his arms.

"Beth."

My name. But the voice was distant, and her words were lost.

"Beth!"

She smiled, and fingers pressed against her lips. Her fingers, warm and damp. His fingers on her forehead.

Hello? But she spoke only in her head, the words flashing against her brain, bright gold against a deep grey emptiness. *Don't go.*

Silence, and the fear overtook her. Alone, she would float away. No one to keep her safe, no one to tie her down, free to fly, free to crash. Crash—and burn, as the car had burned.

As her head burned, raging hot, flames licking her body and, alone, no one would notice, no one would save her and she would burn.

"Beth . . ."

But she wasn't alone. He was still there. His arms. His heartbeat. His face, too bright for her to see. His voice, familiar, indistinct. She had lost his name, lost herself, but he would find her. He would keep her safe.

And the world faded out.

"That is *disgusting!*" Miranda cried, puckering her cheeks and reaching frantically for a glass of water. She took a swig, then another to wash the taste of Kane's scotch out of her mouth. "You can't drink that."

"Not only will I drink it, but for your viewing pleasure, I'll drink it in a single gulp." Kane had whisked her out of the restaurant and taken her to an enormous bar that looked like the inside of an airport terminal. What it lacked in ambiance, it made up for in mug size.

"Not possible," Miranda decreed, glancing skeptically at Kane's oversize glass filled with Glenlivet aged to taste-bud-killing perfection.

"Wanna bet?"

Miranda nodded. "I win, you answer a question. Any question."

Kane rolled his eyes "Remind me to bet you more often. And if I win . . . well, since you've chosen truth, I guess I'll take dare."

"Dare me to what?"

"To be decided later. After I win. You in?"

Miranda glanced down at the glass again, then up at his cocksure face. "I'm in."

Kane shrugged. "Your funeral." He slapped his palm down on the table and, with his other hand, grabbed the glass, tipped his head back, and poured the scotch down his throat. Just before the glass emptied, a spasm of coughing wracked his body, and he spit out the final mouthful—right in Miranda's face.

"I was wrong," she said wryly as she dried herself off with a soggy napkin. "There is something more disgusting than *drinking* scotch."

"I don't get it," Kane mumbled.

"Well, when you spit liquor in someone's face, it is traditional to apologize," Miranda explained. "I know it's a difficult and foreign ritual to understand, but maybe you should just go with it—"

"No, I mean, I never lose," he complained. "There must be something wrong with this glass. And you distracted me, Stevens."

"Yes, I've oft been told that my beauty is enough to drive men to distraction," she joked. "Now, back to business. The question."

Kane sighed and leaned back in his chair, still looking confused. "Fire away."

Under ordinary circumstances, she wouldn't have had the nerve, but she was a little tipsy and even more exhausted, and the combination made her brave. "Why'd you really ruin my date?"

"I told you already, Stevens, the guy was a jerk—"

"Yes, but what made that your problem? I'm sure you've got plenty of things you could have been doing tonight. Why waste your time rescuing me from the dangers of a three-course meal?"

"I don't know what you want me to say," he shot back. "I already told you everything."

"Were you . . . jealous?"

Kane leaned forward, and the sulky expression melted away. His eyes narrowed, and his lips pulled back to reveal gleaming white teeth; everything about the look screamed *challenge.* "And what if I was?"

"Well . . ." She didn't have an answer for that one. In her mind, she hadn't gotten past asking the question. "I don't . . . uh . . ."

"That's what I thought." He looked down at his watch. "It's 12:58," he told her. "You know what that means."

"You have somewhere better to be?"

"It means it's officially tomorrow." He clinked her glass. "And you're officially eighteen. Happy birthday, Stevens. Ready for your present?"

"You didn't have to—"

But she stopped speaking, somehow knowing what he was going to do before he did it. So when his face came toward her, she was expecting it, and when his lips touched hers, she was ready—but that couldn't keep her from getting swept away.

When Beth opened her eyes again, she was lying with her head on Adam's lap, and his arms were still around her. This time, she knew him. "Hey," she said weakly. "What happened?"

"Beth?" He peered down at her nervously, his face crinkled with concern. "Are you—do you know who I am?"

"Of course." She tried to sit up but, still a little woozy, fell back against his side. He held her steady, his grip firm. "How did I get here?" For a moment, she wondered if the last several months had been a long nightmare from which she was finally waking, safe in Adam's arms. But then she remembered—running away from Reed, talking to someone outside the hotel, taking . . . something.

It was all real. Her acts; her lies.

"I didn't know what happened to you. I found you in the alley," Adam said, sounding sick and broken. "And you were . . . it wasn't good."

"Nothing happened. I—I took something," Beth admitted. She rested the back of her hand against her throbbing forehead. "It was stupid. But I think . . . I think I'm okay." She didn't feel okay. She felt weak and shaky, scared that if she didn't hold tight to each word, her thoughts would fly away again, stranding her in darkness and confusion. She couldn't go back there again.

"I was worried." Adam hugged her and pressed his cheek against the top of her head. The pressure felt like an iron barbell, but Beth didn't say anything. Pain or not, she liked knowing he was there. "You really scared me."

"I scared myself," she said, trying to laugh it off. But there was no relief in her voice. As her mind woke up, so did her memory. Not just of the night, but of the year—everything was equally sharp, as if it had all happened at the same time, was still happening. Adam, calling her a slut. Harper, tearing away everything that meant anything to her. Kaia sleeping with Adam. And the rage, the terrible rage that had swept through her and driven her to get revenge. Kaia's death. Reed's pain. Beth's lie.

It was all jumbled in her mind, screaming for attention, and a part of her longed to be back in the silent dark.

"Hey, what is it?" Adam stroked her face, and Beth realized she was crying. She shook her head, but didn't want to speak. She didn't know what would come out.

"I can't tell you," she whispered. "I can't tell anyone."

"You can tell me anything." He wiped away another tear from her cheek. "Is it Reed? Did he . . . do something?"

"No!" She jerked her face away from him. "It was me. I did . . . it doesn't matter now. I can't change anything."

"Maybe I can help."

Beth wanted to laugh. It was such a genuine offer, and such a pointless one. No one could help her, not now. No one could change what she'd done. She searched for the words that would convince him she was okay, so that he could go on with his night and stop showering her with even more care and attention that she didn't deserve. She knew it should only make her feel worse, and hated that it didn't.

In fact, he was helping just by being there. Holding her.

Then the room door swung open—and he let go.

"Harper!" he cried, pulling away from Beth and jumping to his feet. "Oh, shit!"

"It's lovely to see you, too," Harper drawled, her eyes skimming over Beth. They paused only for a second, but it was long enough. Beth could feel Harper's gaze slicing into her, peeling back all her layers until she was left exposed, naked, a shivering mass of raw pain. Harper's expression didn't change, and she moved on.

"I didn't mean that," Adam babbled, "I just meant, I was surprised to see you here—".

"Of course you were, since we were meeting up there," Harper pointed out. There was a strange note in her voice, Beth realized. Something almost human. Almost like . . . pain. "Of course, I was surprised too . . . when you didn't show. But now I get it. You found a better option." She glared at Beth, her eyes narrowed and her teeth bared. "I didn't mean to interrupt—I'll just grab my jacket and get out of your hair."

"It's not like that, Harper, I just forgot, and—"

"Oh, *that* makes me feel a *lot* better. I'm standing up there like an idiot, waiting around, wondering if you were dead or something, because surely nothing but that would have kept you away, not after all that 'I'll never lose you again' *crap.*"

"It wasn't crap," he said quietly.

"Good luck explaining that to your new girlfriend."

"That's not what's going on here," he insisted. "If you'd just give me a chance . . ." Beth expected him to move toward Harper, to do *something*, to force her to understand. But, instead, he just remained where he was, standing in front of the bed, his arms dangling loosely, one of them still brushing Beth's shoulder.

"I *gave* you a chance, and you *forgot,*" Harper snapped.

"That's not fair!"

"You want to talk *fair?* You want to sit *here*, with *her*, and talk *fair?*"

"I don't even know why—"

"STOP!"

Beth wondered why they had both frozen and turned to stare at her. Then she realized that she was the one who had screamed.

She couldn't stand it anymore; she couldn't ruin anything else with her lies and her cowardice. Everything was falling apart around her, and all this destruction, all this pain, it was because of her. She was done. Whatever had happened to her tonight, whatever she had taken, it had apparently had an effect. The terror was still there, but it was quieter, farther away, like her mind had sunk into a deep sea, and all the excuses, all the rationalizations, all the terrifying consequences were muffled by the dark, still waters.

She couldn't stand the twisted pain on Adam's face and the hatred in Harper's eyes, and she couldn't stand her own weakness. Not anymore.

"Adam's only here with me because I lied to him," Beth said. She barely spoke above a whisper, but there must have been something in her voice, or in her face, that commanded attention. Harper and Adam didn't interrupt; they barely moved. "If he knew the truth, he would—" She held her breath until the urge to sob passed. "He would hate me. He should hate me."

Adam still didn't speak, but he sat down again on the edge of the bed and took her hand, pressing it gently. Beth wanted to pull away, but speaking was hard enough. She couldn't move. "I lied to everyone. At least, I didn't tell the truth. Harper, I didn't tell you what happened, and now you think that it was your fault and I wanted to tell you, I did, because I am *so* sorry, even if that sounds stupid and small to say, it's true, I would do anything to change what happened, and if I could I would you have to believe that—"

"*Beth!* What the hell are you talking about?" Harper's hand was trembling, and Beth wondered if some part of her already knew.

It didn't make it any easier to say it out loud.

Beth allowed herself a moment to hope that speaking the truth would change everything: It would lift the cloud of guilt and let her breathe again. It would make up for what she'd done, *redeem* her so that she could enjoy her life again, allow herself to be happy. Maybe it wasn't just a cliché—maybe the truth really would set her free.

The moment passed. And it didn't matter, not anymore. Maybe nothing could save her now. But she had to try.

"I did it." In her mind, Beth delivered the news standing up, facing Harper with strength and dignity, a noble image of apology and disgrace. In reality, she pressed her face into her hands, her shoulders shaking with suppressed sobs, her nose stuffed, her cheeks wet, her voice muffled. "I spiked your drink, Harper. Before the speech. Before the accident." A wave of nausea swept through her, and she fell forward, her head spinning like she was going to pass out. Hunched over, she couldn't see Harper's reaction, didn't even know if Adam was still by her side. A dull, roaring thunder filled her ears. She couldn't even hear her own voice, and wasn't sure if she was speaking at all anymore, or whether she was confessing in her own head.

Maybe, she thought, as the world spun around her, fading in and out of a gray mist, this is all still just a dream.

Still, she forced the words out. Each one hurt, as if scraping a razor blade across her tongue on the way out.

"It was me."

She was no longer in the hotel room; she was back at school, a small pill warm in her hands, slipping into a mug of coffee. Dissolving. Disappearing.

"I did it."

She was on an empty road, standing over a scorched patch of ground, everything matted down. Burned out. Dead. She choked on an acrid stench of smoke and gasoline.

"I killed Kaia."

She stopped waiting to wake up.

chapter

10

First came the relief.

Then came the rage.

Harper pressed herself flat against the wall, her nails digging into the cheap paint. She imagined they were digging into Beth's big blue Bambi eyes. She wanted to claw them out.

I didn't kill her. Every night as Harper went to sleep, she felt her hands on the steering wheel; she heard the crunch of metal, and the screams. But all of it had been a lie. It might as well have been Beth at that wheel; it might as well have been a gun in Beth's hand. *It wasn't my fault,* Harper thought in wonderment.

It was hers.

"I don't . . . I don't understand," Adam stuttered. Harper realized he was still sitting next to Beth on the bed—next to a killer. Their hands were clasped together. She held herself still, and tried to resist the urge to attack. "How could you . . . what do you mean you killed her?" Adam said. "You weren't even there, and—I thought Kaia was driving the car?"

"I was driving," Harper said flatly. The words had been trapped in her for so long, poisoning everything. And now they didn't even matter.

And Beth had known all along, she realized. Beth had known, and let Harper believe . . .

She almost hadn't survived the guilt. She had almost drowned. And Beth held the life preserver in her arms, saw her flailing—and turned away.

"I was driving," she said again, louder this time. The words gave her power. "But this—" Bitch. Psycho. Murderer. "*You*. You put something in my drink. And you let me get up there in front of all those people and make an ass of myself. Then you let me get into a car. You just let—" She gasped, remembering the sirens, remembering the screams. "You just let it happen."

"I'm sorry . . . !" Beth wailed, her words trailing off into an incoherent moan. She tipped over onto her side and curled up into a tight fetal ball, shaking. Adam leaned over her, stroking her head.

"What the hell are you doing?" Harper asked Adam. "Didn't you hear her? She *killed* Kaia. And she let me think that I—what are you doing?"

"We have to give her a chance to explain," Adam said softly, as if Beth were a child who'd just confessed to breaking Harper's favorite lamp. "This doesn't make any sense, and she . . . it's *Beth*. She's a good person. There must be some explanation, some—"

"There's nothing!" Harper shrieked. She felt like she'd slipped into some parallel universe where everyone but her was insane. How could he not see what was going on, and who he was comforting? How could he not care what she'd done to Kaia—to *Harper*? "There's no excuse. There's nothing she can say. She did it. She deserves to cry. She deserves to be miserable. She deserves to go to hell, and you should leave her the hell alone."

Adam looked at her helplessly. "Don't say that. I can't. She's still . . . whatever she did, I still care about her. I can't just leave her here, like this." He rubbed his hand slowly across Beth's heaving shoulders. She didn't appear to notice.

Harper's stomach contracted, and tears of rage sprung to the eyes. Adam was a caring, responsible guy. It was one of the reasons she loved him. But this was ridiculous. He was *Harper's* best friend—or he was supposed to be. He was supposed to love her. Protect her. Support her.

He was supposed to be on Harper's side. But here he was, embracing the enemy.

"I made a mistake," Harper reminded him, "because I *loved* you—and you threw me out of your life. You told me I was a horrible person, that you could never trust me again. Because I made a fucking mistake. But she . . . she *kills* someone, and you just . . . shrug?" Harper forced her voice not to tremble. She walked slowly to the door, turning away from Adam and placing her hand on the knob. "If you ever cared about me, you wouldn't be able to look at her. You'd leave her here to rot. You'd leave right now."

"Don't say that, Harper," Adam pleaded. "Please. Don't make me . . ."

Don't make me choose. That's what he'd been about to say. And a chasm of black, bottomless darkness opened up

inside Harper. Because if he thought he had to choose—
if he thought, now, after hearing the truth, that there
was a choice, that he had any option but one—then it was
already over.

"She needs someone right now, Gracie. I can't leave her
alone."

I *need you,* Harper thought bitterly. But she didn't say
it out loud. He shouldn't need to hear it. "I'm leaving.
Come if you want. Stay if you want."

Harper opened the door, stepped through, and closed
it behind her.

She didn't need to look back to know what he'd
decided.

Adam couldn't believe she was gone.

He couldn't believe any of this. Things like this didn't
happen. Not to him.

He was having trouble processing. Beth had spiked
Harper's drink. Harper had gotten into the car. And Kaia
had—

None of it made any sense. Beth was so gentle, such a
good person, always doing the right thing, guiding him in
the right direction. He'd been with her for almost two
years, and he knew what kind of person she was. The kind
that would never do anything like this. Never.

Unless she'd been pushed past her breaking point.
Unless something had happened—some *one* had pushed
her so hard, hurt her so badly, that she'd broken.

Maybe me. He remembered pushing her away, cursing
her, hating her for something she hadn't done. He remembered sleeping with Kaia—and breaking Beth's heart.

He looked down at Beth, who was sobbing into the comforter, her hands balled up tight and thumping softly against the bed, her eyes squeezed shut. She needed him.

But what if he needed Harper?

He owed Harper his loyalty. He owed Beth his help, maybe even his forgiveness. What did he owe himself?

"Leave me alone," Beth mumbled, her arm spasming out as if to shoo him away. "You shouldn't be here."

Adam knew that he should, and that whatever Beth said, she knew it too. But he couldn't stop staring at the door. And, eventually, he couldn't stop himself from standing up, walking over, and opening it.

He looked up and down the hallway. Only a few minutes had passed, but he had waited too long. She was gone.

She probably hadn't gone far—he was sure he could find her. But he could still hear Beth weeping, back in the room. She was crushed. Damaged. Helpless. And Adam still cared about her, enough to cringe at her whimpering. Enough to want to hold her and give her comfort, maybe even forgiveness, if that's what it would take.

"Shhh, I'm back," he told her, gathering her up in his arms.

"No."

"Yes. And I'm not leaving you."

Beth was weak, and she needed him *now*. Harper was strong.

She could wait.

The kiss hadn't lasted long enough.

One moment he'd had his arms around her, his lips pressed to Miranda's, his eyes closed while hers stared, wide open, memorized the tiny dips and crinkles in the skin around his left eye. The next moment, which came far too quickly, Kane had pulled away, and they were seated across from each other again, as if nothing had happened.

Maybe nothing had, and her obsession with Kane had finally swept away her last grip on reality. But she didn't think so.

What did it mean?

Nothing?

Everything?

She was afraid of the answer, reluctant to ask. Harper saved her the trouble.

"Thank God you're here!" she cried, flinging her arms around Miranda. "I don't know what to do. I don't know what just happened. I just, I don't knoooooooow."

Miranda let her best friend cry against her shoulder, trying not to regret the fact that she'd left Harper a message to explain where she was or to wonder whether her brand-new, now-tear-stained birthday shirt was dry-clean-only. She certainly tried not to resent the fact that Harper's latest melodrama was interrupting—well, she didn't know what it was, but that was the point.

Above all else, Miranda was a good friend, and good friends listened. They sometimes snuck glances out of the corner of their eye at tall, well-built Greek gods in training, and sometimes got distracted wondering how to kiss that hot smirk off a certain hot face—but mostly, they listened. Or at least pretended to.

"What's wrong now?" Miranda asked, lightly patting Harper's back.

And then Harper began to tell her story, and as the

details poured out, Miranda no longer needed to pretend.

"Kaia's dead, and now Beth's just lying there, crying, like *I'm* supposed to feel sorry for *her*," Harper concluded, taking a long gulp of Miranda's drink and then, finishing it, grabbed Kane's out of his hand and downed that one too. "And Adam's just taking it. Like he doesn't care. That she *killed* someone. That she drugged me. That . . ." Harper sagged against Miranda, moaning as if all the words had leaked out of her. Then she burst into tears.

"I don't believe it," Miranda said, shaking her head.

"I do." Kane had been so silent that Miranda had almost forgotten he was there. He was holding himself very still, his fingers pinching the bridge of his nose. "I should have known," he said, so quietly that she could barely hear him. "I should have figured it out."

"But it doesn't make any sense," Miranda countered. "Where would she even get the drugs, and how would she, how could she do something so . . ." But she was beginning to remember how it had felt, those days and weeks after Harper betrayed her—and how Beth's pain had cut so much deeper. How Beth's lust for revenge had overwhelmed them both. And Miranda had been more than happy to let Beth talk her into anything. She had so desperately wanted to lash out, to hurt Harper the way she'd been hurt. If Beth had come to Miranda with the plan— the plan she must have thought would be harmless— would Miranda have talked her out of it?

Or would she have gone along for the ride?

Harper didn't know how long she had been crying. She'd held it together as she walked out of the hotel room, strode down the hall, waited impatiently for the elevator—maybe because she had still hoped Adam would follow.

But he didn't. And when the elevator doors closed her in, she lost it. She'd been crying ever since. Crying and drinking, drinking and crying, and even though she was in public, and she could feel Miranda and Kane staring down at her, for once, she didn't care. What did it matter what they thought—what anyone thought?

She was in a strange city, surrounded by foreign people and places, and her world was shattered.

It shouldn't matter, she told herself. Losing Adam. She'd been through worse. She'd lost more than that. She'd survived.

But it all added up. And just knowing what Beth had done, knowing she was up there in the room, with Adam, that the two of them were . . . together . . . it felt like a knife digging into her side, carving out pieces of flesh. Soon there would be nothing left.

She felt a light touch on her shoulder. At least she still had Miranda. She felt a gush of gratitude. "Harper, come on, let's get out of here," her friend—the only one who *hadn't* betrayed her—said gently.

"I can't go back to the hotel," Harper moaned. "Not when he's there. With her."

"Okay. Okay, then, let's just go somewhere more private, get you . . . cleaned up."

Dimly, Harper realized she must look like shit. And probably the whole bar was staring at the crazy girl, wondering what was wrong with her.

Someone spiked my drink, Harper thought giddily. *Call the cops.*

She didn't care about any of it, but she let Miranda pull her out of the chair and guide her toward the back of the bar. Kane kept his hand on her lower back, keeping her steady. She wanted to tell him she didn't need his help, but she couldn't choke the words out.

"I'm going to take her in here," Miranda said, and Harper realized she was talking to Kane. She was talking as if Harper couldn't hear her, couldn't speak or act for herself.

Miranda pushed open the door to the women's room, and Kane caught Harper's hand, pulling her toward him. He placed a hand on each of her shoulders and held her firmly. He looked blurry and out of focus, but she knew it was just the tears. "We'll figure this out, Grace," he said. "It's all going to be fine."

He'd always been a good liar.

Miranda led her inside the empty bathroom and left Kane outside to guard the door. Harper, usually unwilling to touch anything in a public restroom without several layers of paper towel between her and the germs of the masses, hopped up on the edge of the sink and leaned back against the mirror.

"This is it," she said dejectedly, trying to pull herself back together. "He's gone. I have to deal."

"He's not gone," Miranda pointed out. "He's back in the room right now, probably wondering where you are. You sure he didn't call you?"

Harper shrugged. He had called. Seven times. She hadn't answered. "I don't care if he's looking for me. He stayed with her, after what she did. He *stayed with her.*"

"Is that really so unforgivable?"

"Rand, after what she did to me?"

"She didn't do it to *you*," Miranda said flatly. A look of horror flashed across her face. "I'm sorry, I didn't mean it to sound like—"

"Yeah. You did." Harper hung her head down and wiped away the last of her tears. "I get it. I'm selfish. It's all about me. Whatever. This isn't about me, I get that. It's about Kaia. No, screw that. It's about Beth, and what she did—and how she lied about it. She hurt so many people, Rand. And a few little tears and it's like, *poof*! Adam forgives and forgets. He never forgave *me*."

"I know." Miranda put an arm around Harper's shoulders. "I know it feels like he's choosing Beth over you—"

"Because he *is*," Harper said sullenly. At least she was finally getting it.

"But maybe . . ."

"What?"

Miranda opened her mouth. Shut it again. "Never mind."

"Just tell me!"

"Maybe it's not as simple as you're making it out to be," Miranda suggested.

"She spiked my drink because she wanted to humiliate me. She wanted to ruin my life, and ended up killing Kaia. She's a *murderer*. What's simpler than that?"

"But she didn't *mean* for it to happen." Miranda smoothed Harper's hair down and rubbed a hand across her back. "It was an accident."

Harper laughed bitterly through her tears. "An accident. Right. The only accident is that Kaia's the one who ended up dead. You know the little psycho was hoping it was me."

Miranda sighed. "No. She didn't want you dead. She just wanted . . ."

"What are you, a mind reader now? How could you know what she wanted? She's crazy. She's evil. She *wanted* me dead. And she almost got it."

Miranda took a deep breath. "Harper, I think all Adam's trying to do is look at it from her side. He's not betraying you. He's just . . . well, imagine what she must have been feeling—what could have made her do something so stupid."

"What the hell are you trying to say?" But it was obvious. Harper would never have thought Miranda would have the nerve for bullshit like this. Kane, maybe. But not Miranda. Never Miranda. But if this was where she wanted to go, Harper was damn well going to make sure she went all the way. "Do you mean *what* made her—or *who* made her?"

"She was hurting," Miranda said. "And . . . I can kind of imagine how she felt." Harper could tell from her expression that Miranda was remembering her own pain; she was remembering her own anger. At Harper. "Maybe she just wanted to strike back, hurt someone the way she—"

"Maybe I *deserved* it," Harper snapped. "That's what you're trying to say, isn't it? Maybe you agree with her— maybe *you* wish I was the one who'd died!"

Miranda flinched, and her lip began to quiver the way it always did just before she started to cry. "Don't say that. You know that's not what I mean. I'm not trying to hurt you." She tried to touch Harper again, but wised up when she caught the look on Harper's face. She stepped away. But she refused to stop. "I know you don't want to believe this. I know you want it to be simple, and have Beth be evil, and everyone on your side—"

"Because that's the truth," Harper insisted. "That's reality."

"Or maybe that's just what you want to be true, because then you wouldn't have to face the fact that maybe you—"

"You want to talk about what's true?" Harper said, hopping off the sink and charging toward Miranda. She couldn't let the conversation go any further—she didn't know what would happen if she let Miranda finish her thought. "*You're* going to tell *me* about making my own reality? Avoiding the harsh glare of truth?" She forced a bitter laugh. "That's hilarious. That is fucking hilarious."

"Harper, I'm just trying to—"

"And here, of all places." Harper spun around, flinging her arms out toward the filthy stalls. The anger coursing through her felt good. It swept away the misery, and gave her strength. Power. "You think I don't know what you're doing, rushing off to the bathroom after every meal? You think I haven't figured out your pathetic little problem, even if you want to pretend it doesn't exist?"

"That's ridiculous, Harper, I do not—"

"What was that about facing the truth? Oh, 'I don't want to hurt you,'" Harper said, pouring a bucket of fake sympathy into her voice, "'but it'll be *good* for you to face reality.' Life isn't always what you *want* it to be, after all. You want to be sexy, desirable, and stick thin—but instead all you are is a pathetic closet-case bulimic who's so incompetent at keeping your oh-so-special secret that the whole world knows what a head-case you are."

"Harper, stop it," Miranda whispered, backing away. "Please."

"And if you want to talk hard truths, here's another one," Harper yelled. "Kane will never love you. He knows how you feel, and he's playing with you. Like a toy. Get it? You're a joke to him. You're nothing."

Harper wanted to stop herself now. She'd gone too far. She pressed her hand against her lips, to stop the flood of words. But the dam wouldn't hold for more than a second. Screaming at Miranda, forcing the tears out of her, was the only way to drown out everything that Miranda had said. And everything she hadn't said.

Because Harper could fill in the blanks.

You wouldn't have to face the fact that maybe you caused this. Beth would never have done it, if it hadn't been for you.

Kaia might still be alive if it hadn't been for you.

You destroyed everything good in Beth's life—what did you expect her to do?

You still got in the car. You're still the one who was behind the wheel.

"Shut up!" she screamed, even though Miranda hadn't said anything. "You've been following after Kane like a sick little groupie for all these years, and where has it gotten you? You're alone, you're bitter, and you puke your guts out every day like the before version of some Oprah charity project. And you want to lecture *me* about avoiding the truth? You make me sick."

Miranda fled, flinging open the door—and slamming into Kane, who was waiting just outside. It was obvious he'd heard everything. She took one look at him, let out a thin cry of despair, and ran away. "Miranda!" he called. "Wait—" But she kept running.

Kane stared after her for a moment, then turned

slowly toward Harper. "How could you?" he asked, his voice icy.

She just wanted to crawl into a corner and die. "Kane, I—"

"Don't." He'd never looked at her that way before: stern and serious. Disappointed. "Just don't." And he spun around and left her behind.

Harper gulped in one deep breath after another, trying to summon up the strength to figure out what to do.

She needed to do *something*. She needed to fix this, fix everything. But it was all so screwed up. How could all of her friends turn on her like that—why couldn't they see that Beth was the enemy? Why were they so ready to give her their sympathy and to leave Harper to fend for herself?

You drove them away, a voice in her head pointed out.

But that wasn't what she wanted to hear. She wanted to hear someone rage against Beth for what she'd done. She wanted to hear that she wasn't the only one who cried herself to sleep most nights, imagining that she could still hear Kaia's icy laugh.

Or Kaia's screams.

She wanted someone to blame for everything that had happened. She wanted someone to punish.

And though her friends may have abandoned her, she suddenly realized that she wasn't alone.

It took a few phone calls and a little detective work, but in Grace, CA, there were far fewer than six degrees of separation between Harper and, well, anyone. She had the phone number in under five minutes. It only rang once.

"Beth?" a voice asked hopefully. "Where did you—"

"It's not Beth," she snapped. "Is this Reed?"

"Yeah, but who—"

"This is Harper Grace. We need to talk."

Sleep was impossible. But Beth had gotten good at pretending. She lay on her side, Adam's arm curled protectively around her, his face pressed against her shoulder, and kept her eyes closed, listening to his steady breathing. Her arm was twisted at an odd angle and had long ago fallen asleep; her neck ached, and she longed for a tissue with which to blow her stuffed-up nose or to clean the dried tears off her face. But she didn't want to move, lest she wake him.

She didn't want him to leave.

Because she was so intently focused on Adam—the comforting pressure of his body, the soft, snuffling sounds he made as he slept, the tickle of his hot breath on her neck—she didn't hear the door inch open, or the footsteps creep toward the bed. And because she had her eyes closed, she didn't see the figure standing over her, fists clenched.

But she smelled him. Stale coffee, cigarettes, motor oil, and the faint sweetness of fresh-grown marijuana. She squeezed her eyes shut even tighter, hoping he would believe the pose and go away, so she wouldn't have to face him—not like this.

"Is this a fucking joke?" he growled loudly.

Adam jerked awake and stared groggily at the intruder. Beth opened her eyes and sat up, wondering how much he knew, and how much she would have the courage to tell him.

"We fell asleep," she lied. "But nothing happened. Adam was just—"

"You think I give a shit what you do with him?" Reed's voice, usually so warm and slow, pelted her like hail, rapid and unforgiving. "You can screw every guy in town, for all I care. You can fucking *die*, for all I care."

And she knew that he knew.

"Don't talk to her like that," Adam said, about to stand up. Beth put a hand on his back.

"Let me," she told him. This was her battle to lose. "Reed . . ." Her voice sounded strangled. Which is how she felt. "I wanted to tell you myself—"

"I *comforted* you," he spit out, looking disgusted. "I touched you, I held you, I let myself—" He sagged against the wall and wiped the back of his hand against his mouth, as if to wipe the memory of her off his lips.

"How did you find out?" she asked in a whisper.

Harper stepped through the open door. "I told him." She glared smugly at Adam. Beth didn't turn to see his reaction. She didn't care about anything right now but making Reed understand.

"It was an accident," she told him, the tears returning even though she thought she'd wept herself dry. "It was a mistake. I should have told you. I know. But . . ."

"But you didn't."

"Because I thought you'd hate me!" she cried.

"You were right."

"Reed . . ." Beth lunged toward him, then, pulling him toward her, wrapped her arms around him and clutched his worn cotton T-shirt in tight fists so he couldn't escape. She expected him to push her away, but he didn't move, just stood there in her embrace, his arms at his sides, his head staring straight ahead over her shoulder, motionless, like a mannequin. She glanced over at Harper, hating to do this in front of her. But she had no choice. "Up on the roof, I only ran away because—because I was afraid of this. I told you! I told you I didn't deserve you, that you didn't really know me. . . ."

"So this is my fault for not believing you?"

"No! No, that's not what I mean." She clutched him tighter and closed her eyes again, trying to memorize everything about his body, knowing this might be her last chance. "I just don't want you to think that I was . . . I wanted to stay with you. I didn't want any of this to happen. I wanted to tell you . . ." She lowered her voice so that only he would hear. "I'm in love with you, too."

There was no answer.

"Reed? Did you hear me? I *love* you. And maybe we can find a way—"

He didn't push her away, or touch her at all, but somehow he stepped out of the embrace, so quickly that Beth found herself holding empty air.

"You make me sick." His voice was hoarse and expressionless. "There's no way. There's nothing."

"But after everything we—"

"Don't you get it? There *is* no we. None of it happened—none of it was real. It was all a lie."

"It wasn't! You have to believe me," she begged, "it was all real. And everything I said was true, except—"

"You're a liar," he said flatly. "You're a killer. You . . . you took her away from me, and then thought you could just *replace* her? You're psychotic."

"I love you," she told him again, this time loud and clear. She knew now that it didn't matter, that he was already gone, but she needed to say the words. She needed them to hang in the air so that there was at least some record of the last good thing in her life, before it faded away.

"I don't even know you," he shot back. "I don't want to." He pressed his hand over his eyes and hunched forward, as if he were struck by a sudden sharp pain. Beth moved toward him again, but Harper was quicker. She materialized by his side; he took her hand.

Beth felt like her own hand had been dipped in acid.

"I'm sorry," she said again, the words now sounding meaningless even to her.

"Save it," Harper sneered, leading Reed to the door. She was no longer holding his hand; now her arm was loosely wrapped around his waist. Beth didn't want to look, but she couldn't help herself. "No one wants to hear your lame apologies." Harper paused in the doorway and glared once again at Adam. "Some things are unforgivable."

chapter

11

Sex on the Beach.

Tequila Sunrise.

Alabama Slammer.

Cosmopolitan.

Appletini.

Mojito.

Kamikaze.

The city was drowning in cocktails, and Harper planned to try them all. The world tipped and turned, spun and sloshed, and she poured another drink down her throat, and another. She drenched her doubts in tequila, showered her guilt with vodka, poured Captain Morgan rum all over the flames that still burst out of a crumpled car, washed Kaia's wounds in a bath of gin.

Harper wobbled down the Strip, a yard-long margarita in one hand, emptiness in the other. She sucked on the straw. One gulp for Adam, who would never choose her. One for Miranda, who now understood the pain of truth.

And the rest for Kaia, who'd left her behind to face it all, alone.

She wobbled. She stumbled. She fell, into the arms of a stranger. His hands were strong, his face gentle, familiar.

"Watch out," he told her, and she'd heard his voice on the radio, she'd seen his eyes on a billboard. She'd longed for this opportunity—in what seemed like another life. "Too much to drink?" the famous addict asked her.

Too much would never be enough.

"No such thing," she mumbled.

"Can I help?"

Front-row tickets, Harper wanted to say. *Backstage passes. For me and my best friends.*

Twenty-four hours ago, it was all she'd wanted. Now she just wanted him to leave her alone. She wanted to forget. She wanted to black out the world.

She wanted another drink.

"I said, can I help?"

She shook her head. The world shook too. The dizziness spun her around, dragged her stomach to her feet. The buzzing in her ears finally blocked out all the words she refused to hear, and a dark fog crowded her vision. She opened her mouth—

And threw up all over the famous man's leather boots.

She felt better. Empty. And that meant she could start all over again. She held out her glass, slurred out the words.

"Fill 'er up."

"Fill 'er up," Miranda told the man with the ladle. The hot fudge sauce came pouring down over four scoops of coffee mocha ice cream with chocolate chips, rainbow sprinkles,

Heath Bar crumbles, sliced banana, almond crumbles, Oreo wedges, and three Reese's peanut butter cups. Miranda stuck a cherry on top.

Then she dug in.

She sat at an empty table, hunched over her tray, and shoveled the food down her throat. She should, more than anything, put the spoon down, stand up from the table, and walk out of the buffet; she should prove Harper wrong, once and for all. But her fingers still gripped the spoon and the ice cream still filled her mouth, sliding down her throat though she barely tasted its sweetness or noticed the cold.

And when it was done, she would have more. She would pile her tray high with black-bottom brownies, cream-centered doughnuts, oversize peanut butter cookies, chocolate truffles, vanilla wafers, raspberry sherbet, apple pie, strawberry shortcake, rice pudding, Oreo cheesecake, cherry tarts, and a chocolate soufflé.

She would stuff it in, wash it down, smear her face and hands with chocolate, drop crumbs all over her lap, keep her head down to avoid the stares. She would curse Harper for driving her to a piggish extreme, and then she would curse herself for her weakness, her disgusting desires, and the bottomless hunger that showed no mercy and had no end.

And when she stopped, sick and bloated but still starving, still empty, and still alone, she would hate herself even more. She would feel the fat surging under her skin like an insect infestation. Her stomach would twist and spasm and her body would scream in protest, until she submitted to the inevitable.

She would lock herself in a dirty stall. Pull her hair

back into a sloppy ponytail. Lean over the toilet bowl. Promise herself this was the last time. And then stick her finger down her throat.

She could see it all playing out, just as it had too many times before. But even that wasn't enough to make her put the spoon down. Not as long as she could still picture Kane's face or hear Harper's voice.

She knew she would eventually have to figure out what to do next, and face up to her life—and her problems. But in the meantime, she would chew and swallow, chew and swallow, until mouthful by mouthful, she filled herself up.

Blondes and brunettes, C-cups and D-cups, strippers and hookers, showgirls and show-offs, the menu was complete, and available à la carte or as an all-you-can-eat buffet. Vegas wasn't picky, and neither were its women.

But Adam's appetite was gone. He felt gutted, wrecked— like this place had chewed him up and spit him out.

Harper had walked away from him; a moment later, Beth had run. And he'd let them both leave. Because he was an idiot—and now he needed to fix his mistake. He needed to find them.

One blonde, five foot four, bright blue eyes, and snow-white skin.

One brunette, wild curly hair with reddish streaks, a wicked smile, just the right curves.

Two women who wanted nothing to do with him. Lost amidst a sea of others who couldn't get enough.

"Don't look so sad, sweetie."

"Want me to cheer you up?"

"Sure I'm not what you're looking for?"

"I'm all yours, baby."

But he didn't want her. He didn't want any of them. He waded through the redheads, threaded his way through a cloud of blondes, strained to see over the Amazonian warriors of a women's basketball team, all outfitted in lime green tank tops and short-shorts that hugged their tightly muscled thighs.

They were barely people to him anymore, just a moving mass of soft parts and honeyed voices. And yet he watched them all, because somewhere in the crowd of hair and lips and chests and hips, he would find something he recognized—maybe a strand of silky blond. Maybe the curving corner of a smug grin, or a pinkie with a razor-thin scar from a sixth-grade art project gone awry.

They were out there, somewhere, one running away from him, the other running away from everything.

There were hundreds of places they could hide; millions of faces to sift through. And he didn't even know where to start.

He knew he'd been dealt a bad hand—but everything was riding on this one, and he wasn't about to fold.

"Fold." Kane threw his cards down in disgust and moved along to the next table. The games blurred together, and still, he played—he bet, he checked, he passed, he raised, he called, and he lost.

His head wasn't in the game.

He tossed a few chips on the blackjack table. "Hit me." A five of clubs slapped down on the table. "Hit me again." A nine of hearts. "Again." Jack of spades.

Bust.

She meant nothing to him, he told himself. Or at least, nothing much. She was just a girl, an automatic no-value discard in the poker hand of life. He wouldn't let himself get fooled into caring, not again. It was a sucker's bet—the house always won, and losing hurt.

It was why he loved to watch the high rollers throwing their thousand-dollar chips down and walking away with a wink and a shrug. Nothing broke them, nothing even dented. Because they never let the game matter. The good ones chose their table carefully, played the odds, risked only what they could afford to lose, and ditched a cold deck without looking back. It was the only way to play.

"Hit me," Kane said again as the dealer shuffled through a fresh deck. Queen of hearts. "Hit me again." King of spades.

Bust.

The best players—the counters—could play several games at once, shifting their focus from one to the other, never letting the money ride too long or leaving while the deck was still hot. Kane did the same thing—just not with cards.

He kept his options open, and his women wanting more. He could spot a winning bet from a mile away, recognized every tell, knew when to smile, when to kiss, when to get the hell out. He could lay down his money and spin the wheel, because with nothing invested, he had nothing to lose.

And so he never lost.

Miranda should be no different. She was, in fact, that most elusive of bets: the sure thing. She knew his game all too well, yet still wanted to play. Because, like the worst of gamblers—like the degenerate losers who stayed at the table as their chips disappeared, waiting in vain to throw that lucky seven and shooting snake eyes every time—she had hope. She expected the next hand—*her* hand—to be different. She actually thought it was possible to beat the house.

Which should have made it incredibly easy for Kane to clean up, and that was the problem: Beating Miranda—*playing* Miranda—would feel like losing. The danger sign blinked brightly. Once emotions got involved, the game was over. You got distracted, you got sloppy and, much like tonight, you walked away with empty pockets.

Or, if you got very lucky, you hit the jackpot.

Kane hated to admit it, but when it came to Miranda, he couldn't hedge his bets. She was an all-or-nothing proposition. And maybe it was time for him to ante up.

> *You promised all or nothing, babe,*
> *You said our bodies fit.*
> *You lied and tore my heart out,*
> *And I don't give a shit!*

Reed's hand was numb, his fingers stinging, his voice hoarse. He leaned into the mic and beat his guitar into submission, letting the rage and pain and misery churn through him and explode into the air.

> *Love me, leave me, kill me dead.*
> *Your voice is like a knife,*
> *Your tears are mud, your hands are claws.*
> *Get the hell out of my life!*

It hurt. It burned. But he wrapped his voice around the notes and let the words slice and stab at an invisible enemy, and though he wasn't drunk and wasn't high, the world seemed miles down as the music carried him up and out, a wall of sound that sucked him in and blasted him out the other side, enraged, exhausted, spent.

Forget it forget me forget you forget,
See your face and I wish I was blind.
Your love and your hate and your lies and your rage,
And you're driving me out of my mind.

The club had been dark and empty when he arrived—but Starl★la had a key. He played and stomped and sang and raged and she closed her eyes, swaying to the music, her body twisting and waving with the sounds, and though he could block out the world, he couldn't miss her hips and her flying hair and her lips, stained with black gloss and mouthing his words.

And then somehow she was on the stage, her body grinding against his, their hips thrusting together as the chords piled on top of one another. And the feel of her flesh and the grip of her hand around his wrist and her breath on his neck reminded him of everything he wanted to forget—everything he wanted to destroy.

He played louder, he sang louder, but the music fell away and the blessed amnesia of sound disappeared and all he could see was Beth's face, her strangled voice, her tears. He tried to lose himself in the thunder of the guitar and the roar of his own voice, but hers was louder and he had to listen.

Please.

Forgive me.

And then Star*la's hands were on his waist and creeping up beneath his shirt, climbing on bare skin, rubbing his chest, and he laid down his guitar and turned to face her, but he wasn't seeing her.

Her black fingernails scraped against his face; he saw only pastel pink, felt silky skin.

Her black hair whipped across his neck; he saw shimmering gold, like strands of sun.

Her eyes, so dark, almost purple, closed; he saw pale blue irises, wide open, alert. He saw tears.

He closed his eyes and when his lips met hers, Beth's face finally disappeared and her voice faded away, and the rage boiling within him spilled out through his hands and his lips and his body. She shoved him up against the wall and dug her elbows into him, pinning him down, and he sucked her lips and bit her earlobe and she scraped her fingers up and down his back until his skin felt raw.

The wall of sound returned. She was like music, a raging, pumping punk anthem come to life in his arms. She kissed his chest and kneaded his flesh and he needed hers. He wanted to sing—he wanted to scream. Their bodies blended together like a perfect chord, and he let himself forget everything but the ceaseless rhythm, the pounding, pulsing beat.

He let himself get lost.

I once was lost, but now am found, Beth sang to herself, tunelessly. She almost giggled, wavering on the edge of hysteria, stepping back from the ledge just in time. She had been confused for so long. Lost, searching for the right path, the right direction, the first step back toward normalcy, to forgiveness, to sanity. Even, someday, to happiness.

And now she understood. She'd found the path, *her* path. It led to a dead end.

Just like Kaia's.

She had been drowning in self-pity, struggling and flailing, fighting the inevitable. It had been exhausting—and now that it had ended, she realized that fighting had been her first mistake. Exhausted, she had submitted to the hopelessness. And now she was finally at peace.

She leaned against the railing, looking out over the sparkling city. Had it been only hours since she'd stood up here with Reed, then fled, uselessly postponing her fate? She felt like a different person now. Because now she understood.

This is it, she told herself. *This is how it always will be.* And this was what she deserved. Reed's disgust and disdain, his hand in Harper's. It was easier to take than what she had seen on Adam's face: sympathy. Concern. A hint of forgiveness. She couldn't let herself fall into the trap, not again. She couldn't seek comfort, or hope for rescue.

She couldn't change what had happened, and she couldn't save herself. But she could at least end the pain. She gripped the railing and looked down, but it was too dark to see anything but the blinking lights smeared across the landscape.

The first step would be hard.

She wondered if it would hurt. Even if it did, it would be fast, and then it would be over. And that was all she wanted—an ending. She couldn't fight the current, not anymore, and she refused to drag Adam down with her when she finally sank to the bottom.

It would be quiet there. It would finally be over.

And justice would be served.

chapter

12

Saying good-bye didn't take as long as she'd expected.

It was a short list, which only reminded her of how little she was leaving behind.

Beth's fingers didn't even tremble as she dialed in the numbers that would take her straight to voice mail. She couldn't face anyone, but she still needed to say she was sorry, one last time.

"It's Harper. Do your best, and if you're lucky, I might call you back."

Beep.

"Harper . . . this is Beth." She took a deep, shuddery breath. "Please don't hang up before you listen to this. I know you'll never understand what I did, and I know you hate me, so I'm not asking you to forgive me. I just want you to know I'm sorry. More than I can ever say. I—" Her voice caught, and she gripped the phone tighter, fixing her gaze on the horizon and forcing herself to stay calm, make it through. "Just take care of Adam. I-I'm glad he'll have you."

One down. Two to go.

Adam's was easier, somehow, maybe because she was only saying what she'd said so many times before. Or maybe because she hadn't hurt him as badly, and didn't owe him as much.

"Hey, it's Adam, you missed me now, but I'll catch you later."

She sighed a little at the sound of his voice, the light Southern accent infusing each word with the hint of a warm smile. "I'm sorry for all the things we said to each other," she told him, wondering when he would hear her words. "And for all the time we wasted being angry. Maybe if I hadn't been so angry, things would have . . . a lot would have been different. We were really good, Ad, and I just want you to know, whatever happened, I still love you. Not like, you know, the way we were, but I'll always—" She stopped. *Always* didn't mean much. Not anymore. "I just hope you don't forget the way things used to be. Before. And Adam . . . thank you. For tonight and . . . just for being . . . you."

Then she waited. For ten minutes, then twenty. Hoping that it would get easier. But when it didn't, she knew she couldn't wait any longer. Reed had gotten a new cell phone the month before, but rarely remembered to turn it on. "Why bother?" he'd always asked Beth. "The only person I want to talk to is already here." She didn't want to just leave him a message; she wanted to talk to him. Not because she thought she'd be able to change anything—she was past that kind of stupid hope—but just because she wanted to hear his voice again. Even if he was angry, even if he told her again how much he hated her, she wanted to hear him say her name.

He didn't answer.

"You know who it is and you know what you want. Speak."

But Beth didn't know what she wanted. "Reed. Reed . . ." Saying his name was all it took, and she burst into tears. She pressed a hand over the receiver, hoping to muffle her sobs, and quickly choked them back, forcing herself to talk. "It's beautiful here," she said in a thin, tight voice, trying to work up to saying something that actually mattered. "It makes me think of you. It makes me think . . . I'm not sorry, not about us. I shouldn't have lied, and I shouldn't have—I did a terrible thing. I know you hate me. I know you can never forgive me. You shouldn't. I hate myself for what I did to you. But . . . I love you. And I know what I have to do now." She shut her eyes against the lights and tried to picture his face— but all she could see was Kaia. "I can't stand what I did to you, to—" She hiccupped through her tears and had to pause to catch her breath. "What I did to all of you. Not anymore. I'm sorry. For Kaia, and for us. For everything. Just try to remember that—and maybe someday you'll even believe it."

She hung up the phone before she realized that she'd forgotten to say the most important thing of all, maybe because saying it out loud would make it true, and she wasn't ready for that yet. She needed more time. Not much, just a few more minutes of breathing deeply and staring up at the sky and holding on.

A few more minutes, and she would be ready to say good-bye.

Miranda felt sick. The food still churning in her stomach, she could feel the fat moving in, unpacking, making itself at home. She needed to do something about it. But before she could, her phone rang. And, glancing down at the caller ID, she discovered what sick *really* meant.

"Stevens, we need to talk," he said as soon she picked up the phone, giving her an extra couple of seconds to decide what to say. It wasn't enough.

"Kane ... I ..." Her face blazed red just thinking about him and what he'd overheard. There was no way she could face him.

"Meet me back at the hotel, by the pool," he ordered.

There was no way she could disobey.

"Half an hour? You'll be there?" he pressed.

She nodded.

"Well?"

She suddenly realized he couldn't see her through the phone. Thank God. "Yeah. Half an hour." She hung up and, nibbling at the edge of her thumbnail, wondered what would happen next. The options:

He wanted to let her down gently. Which would be humiliating, excruciating.

He wanted to pretend nothing had happened. Which might be better—or even worse.

He wanted to tell her he was madly in love with her, and now that he knew she felt the same way, they could—

She forced herself to stop. She'd promised herself no more lame daydreaming. And it was nearly morning—she was too tired to lie to herself anymore. Kane Geary didn't lurk around in corners, afraid of his feelings, pathetically waiting for a sign.

No, that's me, she thought wryly. When Kane saw what he wanted, he took it.

And he'd already chosen to leave Miranda on the shelf.

She considered ditching him, just sneaking back up to the room and finally getting some sleep. But she never considered it very seriously—doom-and-gloom expectations or not, she needed to know what he wanted. And she needed to prove to herself that she could handle it.

He got there first; maybe he'd already been there when he called. He was sitting on the edge of the pool, his jeans rolled up and his feet dangling in the water. He had his back to her, and Miranda assumed he hadn't seen her come in—but after she'd stood in the entranceway for several long minutes, he called out her name.

"Come here," he urged. "I won't bite."

She slipped her sandals off and sat down next to him, cringing as the unheated water lapped over her toes.

"You just have to get used to it," he told her. "Then it feels good."

"I guess I can get used to anything."

There was about half a foot of space between them, except at their fingertips. Her right hand and his left hand were both pressed flat on the damp cement, less than half an inch apart.

Miranda put her hands in her lap and tried not to pick at her nails.

Silence.

"So," Kane finally said, staring straight out at the water. "Our friends are pretty fucked up, huh?"

Miranda's tension spurted out of her in a loud snort. *Very attractive,* she told herself irritably. *Lovely.*

195

"Yeah." Miranda kicked her feet lightly in the water. "I just can't believe Beth . . ."

Kane tipped his head back, as if to look up at the stars, but they were covered by a reddish haze. "I should have figured it out. Maybe I should have seen it coming."

"If anyone should have, *I* should have," Miranda countered. "I knew how angry she was about what Harper—"

"What *we* did to her," Kane corrected her.

Miranda barely heard. "But I should never have said that to Harper. I thought it would help, but . . . she was so upset and miserable, and I had to go and tell her it was all her fault."

"You didn't tell her that."

"Yeah, but I might as well have. It's what she heard. And it's no wonder she said all those—" Miranda kicked herself. She'd steered the conversation exactly where she didn't want it to go.

"You told her the truth," Kane insisted. "Beth wouldn't have . . . done what she did if . . ."

Miranda shrugged. "But that doesn't mean I had to say it."

"I gave her the drugs," Kane said suddenly, in a very quiet voice. She spun to look at him, and he met her gaze.

"What?"

"I gave her the drugs," he repeated, more steadily. "As a present. I thought . . . it doesn't matter what I thought. I didn't expect her to keep them. Or use them. But I gave them to her. And I helped ruin her life. Hell, I started the whole thing. Which I guess makes me to blame too."

Miranda didn't know what to say.

"Doesn't it?" he asked, his voice rising.

She shook her head, then caught herself. "Yes."

He nodded once and let his head hang low with his chin resting against his chest and his shoulders slumped. It was a pose she'd never seen his body make before, so it took her a moment to identify it: defeat. Miranda lifted her hand and, with painful slowness, reached out for his shoulder. But she stopped, just before she touched him, her fingers trembling. She put her arm down, and they sat in silence.

Something jerked him out of a fitful sleep, but by the time he sat up in bed, whatever it was—the noise, the movement, *something*—was gone. Reed looked around, bleary-eyed and confused. The blinds were mostly drawn, but a thin band of darkness beneath the cheap cotton suggested that morning hadn't yet arrived. His lips were dry and cracked, head foggy, and a sour taste filled his mouth. And the bed was strange, unfamiliar, as was the room. . . .

Oh.

He lay back against the uneven mattress and shut his eyes, as if that could block out the reality he was beginning to remember. He was in Vegas. With Beth. But Beth had—

You're a fool, Kaia's voice told him scornfully. *You fell for it. You fell for* her—*after* me?

He wanted to hate Beth: for Kaia's sake, and for his own. But lying there in the dark, it didn't seem possible. And he hated himself for his failure.

Something began to buzz, and he felt a steady vibration against his hip. His phone, alerting him to a message—its ringing must have woken him up. He flipped it open, and even the dim light of the screen was blinding in the total darkness. There was one voice mail, and as he listened to it, he realized his hand was shaking.

He wanted to hang up in the middle; he wanted to hang up as soon as he heard her voice. But he listened to the whole thing. And he couldn't help but remember: Kaia had left him a voice mail too, once. She had begged his forgiveness. And she had died before he could deliver.

He could picture Beth's face, her lips trembling, tears magnifying her eyes to look like pure blue reflecting pools. She just wanted him to try to understand.

"I can't," he whispered, snapping the phone shut. "I just can't."

"Hey . . . it's the middle of the night," a girl's voice complained. "Go back to sleep." Star*la rolled toward him and draped an arm across his bare chest. She pressed her lips against the nape of his neck, and he felt her tongue darting back and forth, as if tapping out a private message in Morse code. He resisted the urge to push her away.

What did I do? he asked himself silently. But it was a rhetorical question. He remembered everything.

"Sorry I woke you," he murmured, holding himself very still.

"Everything okay?"

He grunted a yes.

"Well, since we're both awake . . ." She began playing with the dark curls of hair on his chest and then, slowly, her fingers began walking their way south. "Want to play?"

Though he didn't want to touch her, he grabbed her hand and tucked it against his chest. "Let's just go back to sleep."

"Mmmm, sounds good." She yawned, then nuzzled into his back; moments later her breathing had settled into a deep and steady rhythm. He dropped her hand and lay quietly with his eyes wide open, staring at nothing. There was something about Beth's message. Something wrong.

I know what I have to do.

Try to remember.

It wasn't his problem anymore; *she* wasn't his problem anymore. Reed closed his eyes and breathed in deeply, counting the seconds. Then breathed out. One. Two. Three. In. One. Two. Three. Out . . .

Sleep would come eventually, he told himself. And if it didn't, there was always the fail-safe option, a small plastic bag with just enough left to help him zone out and forget.

But the voice mail kept replaying itself in his head. Not Beth's—Kaia's.

When he'd gotten Kaia's message, he had thought about calling her back—but decided against it. He would forgive her, he'd already decided. But he wasn't ready to talk to her, not yet. And there had been no hurry.

He'd just assumed they had plenty of time.

When Kane finally lifted his head again, she couldn't read his expression. His eyes were half closed, and his face impassive, hidden in shadow. He rested his hand on her knee and a warm heat radiated out from the point of contact up and down her leg. "Thanks."

"For what?"

"For telling the truth. Like always."

"Kane, I—"

"Stevens, I—"

They laughed, and Miranda gestured that he should speak first.

"I got you something." He pulled a small white, scrunched-up paper bag out of his pocket. "For your birthday. Since you're having such an awesome celebratory weekend so far."

She shrugged. "It's not like it's your fault. It all just happened."

"I am the one who ruined your date," he pointed out.

"Is that a note of *apology* I hear in your voice?" she joked, pressing the back of her hand against her forehead. "Do I have a fever? Because I think I'm hallucinating."

"Shut up and open it," he said, shoving the bag into her hands.

"Lovely wrapping job." She needed the sarcasm. It kept all the real emotions away. Miranda delicately peeled open the mouth of the bag and reached inside, pulling out a necklace of cheap, chunky plastic beads, painted in bright colors and attached to a label marked AUTHENTIC NATIVE AMERICAN JEWELRY. It was about as authentic as an aluminum Christmas tree—and just as tacky. "It's . . . uh . . . nice. Thank you?"

"I saw it and thought of you," he said proudly. "I knew you'd love it."

Miranda knew she probably shouldn't take it as an insult; but, looking down at the garish piece of pseudo-jewelry, it was hard not to. "It was very . . . sweet of you to get me something, Kane. You shouldn't have. I mean, you *really* shouldn't have."

Kane burst into laughter. "Stop looking so appalled, Stevens. I know it's gruesome. It's not like I'm expecting you to like it."

"Oh, thank God." She waved it through the air, giggling as the beads clanked loudly together; wear this and she'd become a human maraca. "But then . . . what's it for?"

"I found it in the gift shop," he explained. "And it reminded me of—"

"The gift shop at the Rising Sun," she cut in. Where they'd spent twenty minutes mocking the jewelry. Kane had strung the ugliest necklace they could find around her neck—and then they'd kissed. "I can't believe you remember that."

"I can't believe *you* forgot."

Miranda didn't want him to know that she remembered every second of that day, that she could show him every point on her skin his hands and lips had touched.

"We picked out a necklace," Kane reminded her, "and I put it around your neck—" He took the garish chain of beads out of her hands and latched it around her neck, pausing as his fingers fumbled with the clasp and brushed against her skin. "Like this. And then we stared at each other." His forearms rested on her shoulders, locking her in. She could see her reflection in his eyes. "Like this. And you got all awkward and sarcastic . . ."

"That's me," she joked, trying to smile, "ruining things like always."

"And I wouldn't let you." He moved closer, never taking his eyes off of hers. "I told you how beautiful your lips are—"

"No, you didn't."

"So you *do* remember," he crowed, raising an eyebrow.

"No, I just know I wouldn't have gone for a lame line like that," Miranda countered.

"Girls love my lines," he said, close enough that she could feel his breath on her lips, close enough that she couldn't see his mouth moving because his enormous, dark brown eyes filled her field of vision.

"I'm different," she reminded him.

"I know. That's why, instead, I just—" And the distance between them disappeared as he kissed her. Everything disappeared other than his lips, and the touch of his skin as she stroked her hand across his cheek. His teeth, nibbling at her earlobe. Her tongue, lightly grazing his neck. His breathing, heavy and fast, her quiet gasp as his warm hand slipped beneath her shirt and pressed against the skin of her lower back.

And then reality came rushing back, and she pushed him away.

Right into the pool.

"Oh, no!" She jumped to her feet as he flailed about, finally finding his footing and standing up in the waist-deep water, drenched. "I can't believe I just did that, I'm so sorry, I—"

"It's fine," he assured her, holding out his hand. "Help me up?"

She should have seen it coming. She'd seen enough movies. But she still took his hand—and, like clockwork, he pulled her in after him. The cold water slapped her in the face, spun her upside down, and when she found the surface, shivering and gasping, she was alert again, aware enough to stay away.

"Now you want to tell me why we're both in the pool?" Kane requested, wading toward her. She backed away.

"You pulled me in!"

"You pushed me first."

"Good point."

Kane sliced through the water and, before she could get away, wrapped his arms around her.

"Let go," she said, and it sounded less like an order than a question.

"You're shivering," he pointed out.

"And you're soaking wet, so I don't see how that's helping."

"Why did you push me away?" he asked, his lips at her ear.

Miranda didn't say anything.

"I thought we were having fun," he prodded. "Weren't you having fun?"

She nodded, even though he couldn't see her face. Her chin dug into his shoulder; he'd get the idea.

"So why push me away?"

"You know why," she said quietly. He was right, she was shivering—but not because of the cold.

"No."

"Yes you do! Please don't make me say it."

"Miranda, I don't . . . ?"

"You heard Harper." She tried to slide out of his embrace, but he wouldn't let her. He only let go a little, so he could see her face. That was worse. "You *know* why I . . ." Miranda just wanted to look away, to *be* away, but the best she could do was squeeze her eyes shut so she didn't have to see him looking at her. "I can't do casual. Not with you. It's too hard."

"And what if I don't want casual?"

She didn't want to understand his meaning, because it was too dangerous. If she was wrong . . .

"Open your eyes, Miranda."

She shook her head.

"Open them, or I'm kissing you again," he threatened.

She opened her eyes.

"Let's try this," he told her. He wasn't smirking, or even smiling. "You. Me. For real. Let's just do it."

"But . . . why?" Was this some kind of pity thing? Didn't he know how much worse that would make everything in the morning, when the dream ended and she woke up?

"Because you want to. And because . . . I want to." He didn't sound sure, but he looked it.

"It would never work."

"Probably not. But Stevens, why not take a chance for once?"

It was easy for him to say. He wasn't the one with everything to lose.

On the other hand . . . what did *she* have to lose, she asked herself, when she had so little to start with?

She'd spent so long convincing herself that this moment would never happen, and now here it was—and she almost hadn't recognized it. She was terrified; but that was no excuse.

"Okay."

"Okay?" he repeated, his irresistible smile finally making an appearance. "You'll deign to give me a shot?"

It was hard for her to speak, since she was barely breathing. "I guess you lucked out. So . . . what now? Should we, uh, talk about what we're going to—"

He pressed his right hand to her lips, then, lightly, traced a path across her cheek, to the tip of her ear, then down along the edge of her jaw, coming to rest with his fingers just beneath her chin. "Enough talking," he told her. "We have a deal—now we celebrate."

The water was still ice cold, but as he leaned down and kissed her, his soaking hair dripping down her face, his wet T-shirt sticking to her skin, she felt perfectly warm.

And though the water was only waist deep and her feet were firmly planted on the floor of the pool, she felt like she was floating.

Beth didn't know why she answered the phone. She supposed it was a reflex, left over from her old life. She couldn't have been hoping that there was still a chance— that someone could say something that would make a difference. Even if there was someone who could reach out to her through the phone and explain to her how to fix things, this wasn't going to be that kind of call.

Beth had seen the number on the caller ID and she picked it up, anyway, but that didn't mean she was ready to talk. She lifted the phone to her ear but remained silent, trying to decide whether to hang up.

"I can hear you breathing." Harper's voice was low and cold. It reminded Beth of someone, though at first she couldn't figure out who. Then it came to her: Kaia. "I know you're there. Beth. *Beth.* Say something."

What do you want? It took her a moment to realize

she'd only mouthed the words, and no sound had come out. She tried again. "What do you want?" It was barely more than a whisper, but it was enough.

"What do I want? What do *I* want?" Beth held the phone away from her ear, but could still hear Harper's tinny laugh. "You're the one who called me, remember? Oh no, wait, you didn't *call* me, you left a message. Like a coward. Afraid to face me, Beth? Too afraid I'll tell you what I really think of you?"

"I think I've got that figured out already."

Just hang up the phone, she told herself, *and you can end this for good.*

"Don't pretend you know what I think," Harper snapped. "If you knew anything, you wouldn't leave some stupid message whining about how sorry you are, like that's going to change anything. You don't get to do that."

"What should I do, Harper?" she asked, trying to sound tough, but failing miserably. "You tell me."

"Grow a fucking spine for once, how about that? You face me. You face me and tell me what you did—"

"I already told you."

"You tell me again, and you tell me how *sorry* you are," she sneered, "and then you listen when I tell you exactly where to stick your useless apologies. *You. Face. Me.*"

"I can't."

"Where are you?"

Beth didn't say anything.

"Where the hell are you!" Harper screamed, the last word sliding into a shriek of rage.

Beth just wanted it to stop; she wanted everything to

stop. "I'm on the roof," she whispered. "At the hotel. On the roof."

"Stay there," Harper commanded in a dangerous voice. "I'm coming."

Beth hung up.

Why? she asked herself, the panic rising. Why tell her, when it would be impossible to face her without disintegrating? Just one more stupid decision in a lifetime of them. Harper would arrive soon, and Beth knew what she would say. And it would all be true. "Coward." "Bitch." *"Murderer."* There would be no one to calm Harper down, and no one to hold Beth and assure her—lie to her—that it would be all right. There was no one left at all. The fear and loneliness threatened to overwhelm her—and then she remembered.

It didn't matter how angry Harper was. It didn't matter what she wanted to say.

Because by the time she got there, it would be too late. It would be over.

chapter

13

The phone call sobered her up. Harper ran the entire way back to the Camelot, fearing that Beth would lose her nerve and disappear. And as she reached the top of the stairs, she discovered she'd been right to worry: The roof was empty.

Screw it, Harper thought in disgust. She should have known better. For all she knew, Beth had never been here in the first place. Maybe she'd thought it would be fun to send Harper on a wild-goose chase. She was probably downstairs in the room—*Harper's* room—right now, enjoying a good night's sleep. Or worse, she was down there awake, and she wasn't alone.

Harper refused to consider the possibility. Not because it wasn't likely, but because she'd done enough vomiting for the night.

She hesitated on the rooftop, trying to plan out her next move, and that's when she saw it: a hint of blond, just behind the walled edge of the roof.

The Camelot rooftop was shaped like a turret, with a flat, round top surrounded by a thin, waist-high wall of fake brick, assembled in a cutout pattern that looked like jack-o'-lantern teeth. The gaps were wide enough to sit on—and low enough to climb through.

Harper took a few quiet steps across the roof, as the tip of a blond head dipped below the brick and then, a few seconds later, bobbed into sight again. It wasn't until Harper reached the opposite end that she got a good view of what was happening: Beth had climbed over the wall and found footing on a narrow ledge that ran around the outside of the turret. She was pressing herself flat against the fake brick, one hand clutching an ugly plaster gargoyle, the other balled into a fist.

"You can do it," she murmured to herself. "Come on. Come on. Do it."

"Holy shit." The words popped out of Harper's mouth before she could stop herself. "Beth, what the hell are you doing?"

Beth twisted her head up to see Harper, who caught her breath, as it looked for a moment that the movement might shift Beth's balance enough to send her flying. "You weren't supposed to see this." She turned away again, and stared down—*way* down—at the ground. "But I couldn't—"

"Then what was the plan, genius?" Harper snapped. "I was supposed to come back here and find you all splattered and bloody on the ground?" Beth flinched, and Harper pressed on. "Yes, splattered and *bloody* what did you think would happen if you do something stupid like this? You float to the ground on a magical cloud and ride off into the sunset? Are you nuts? Oh wait, what am I saying? Look where we are. Of *course* you're freaking nuts."

Stop, she begged herself. *Just shut up. Tell her not to jump. Tell her it will all be okay.* Harper knew her role in this script, and the ineffectual clichés she was supposed to utter. She was supposed to play the hero, to save Beth—and the thought enraged her. Where was Beth when Kaia needed saving?

Where was Beth when Harper was lying on the ground in pain, choking on smoke, waiting for sirens, waiting to hear Kaia scream, or move, or breathe?

"I don't owe you anything," she cried. "Do you hear me? I owe you *nothing!*"

Beth didn't respond. From where she was standing, Harper could see Beth's arm shaking and her grip on the gargoyle slip, then tighten. She could see the tears running down Beth's face, and the way the ball of her left foot stuck out over the edge. And, if Harper leaned over, she could see all the way down, to the half-empty parking lot below. She could see the spot where Beth would land.

If.

Harper wondered if it would be possible to survive a drop like that, and wondered how you would land. If you dove forward, would you smash into the pavement gracefully, like a diver hitting an empty pool, arms first, crumpling into the cement, and then head, then body? Or would you twirl through the air in some accidental acrobatics and fall flat, a cement belly flop? An old Looney Tunes image flashed through her head, and for a second, she pictured a deep, Beth-shaped hole in the ground, Beth standing up and brushing herself off, flat as a pancake but otherwise intact.

This is real, Harper had to remind herself. The edge was real. The drop was real. The ground was real. She could climb onto the wall and all it would take was one step, and everything would end. No equipment necessary. *This is real.*

"Beth. Don't." Her voice had none of the sugary sweetness of some touchy-feely suicide hotline. Harper, in fact, couldn't associate the word "suicide" with this scene—that was a textbook word, a TV word, something ordered and comprehensible that happened to fictional characters and crazy teenagers on some other town's local news. This was too messy to have a label, especially a label that pre-dicted, *required*, a certain end. This was just some nameless thing that was happening, and she wanted it to stop. "Come back up here. We'll talk."

"You don't want to talk to me," Beth said dully.

"Yes, of course, I do."

"You hate me."

"No," Harper protested. Lied. "I forgive you. I accept your apology. Just come back up here. We'll figure it out."

She wanted to mean it, but she couldn't, and it showed. "Look, let me call someone," she suggested. "Reed or—" Even now, she couldn't say it. "Someone."

"No!" Beth twisted around in alarm, again almost losing her grip. "Don't call anyone! And don't lie to me."

You're the liar, Harper wanted to say. The hypocrite, the crusader for truth and justice, the perfect, principled princess, little miss can't be wrong. What a joke—what a fraud she had turned out to be. No one had ever guessed at what lay beneath the blond hair and blue eyes.

But had it always been there? Harper wondered. Or had circumstances created it?

Circumstances. Such a bland, passive, forgiving word. Circumstances, like heartbreak, manipulation, humiliation. Circumstances, as if they were beyond human control. As if, in the end, there was no one to blame.

Circumstances had propelled Beth over the wall, onto the narrow ledge, to the limits of sanity and the cusp of disaster. Circumstances had left only Harper as her would-be savior.

Circumstances, it seemed, were out to get them both.

"What do you want me to say?" Harper asked wearily. "What are you waiting to hear? Can we just cut to it?"

"I know what you're thinking. You're thinking how pathetic I am. I can't even do *this* right."

Harper didn't allow herself to question whether it was true. "You're not pathetic, Beth."

"I said don't lie to me!" she wailed.

"I don't know what else I'm supposed to say here."

"Try the truth," Beth suggested bitterly.

"I can't."

"Because you know what you'd have to say. Because you *want* me to jump."

The unspoken accusation: *You want me to die.*

Harper wanted to deny it. She didn't want to hate anyone that much. Death was too final. She got that now, finally understood that Kaia was never coming back.

But Kaia didn't have to die, she reminded herself. They could call it an accident all they wanted, but that didn't make sense. Nothing so huge, and so horrible, could be so random; it didn't feel right. There had to be a reason—there had to be someone to blame.

And didn't that mean someone should have to pay?

"Let me in!" Reed shouted, pounding harder on the door. "Come on, wake up! Let me in!" Finally, just as he'd accepted the fact that no one was there, the door swung open, Adam in its wake.

"What?"

Now that he was here, Reed almost didn't want to ask the question. What she wanted to do was her business. But he had to make sure. "Is Beth here?"

"What's it look like?" Adam stepped aside and ushered Reed into the empty hotel room. Unless she was hiding in the closet, Beth wasn't there.

He checked, just to make sure. The closet was empty.

"Where is she?" Reed asked.

"Hell if I know. I thought she was with you."

"Why? Did she say something?"

Adam stifled a yawn. "When she ran out of here, I figured she was looking for you. Guess not."

"If you hear from her, can you just tell her to call me?" Reed said, trying to keep the worry out of his voice. "I need to see her."

"Why? So you can mess with her head some more? Maybe get her high again? That worked great the last time. If I hear from her, I'll tell her she's better off without you. Or maybe she's finally figured that out for herself."

Reed wasn't big on physical violence. Especially when it came to all-star athletes who could bench-press cars. But he didn't even stop to think before grabbing Adam's shoulders and pushing him up against the wall. "This isn't a joke. I need to find her."

Adam took a deep breath, then another. "Look, asshole,

you want to take your hands off me," he said, in a deliber-
ate and measured voice. *"Now."*

Reed let his arms drop, and sagged against the door
frame. "If you hear from her. Please."

Adam's scowl shrunk almost imperceptibly. "I'm not
going to hear from her. She's not answering her phone.
But . . ." He grabbed for his cell. "Let me call again and—
shit."

"What?"

"There's a message—I must have fallen asleep, missed
the call. Hold on." He dialed into his voice mail, his eyes
widening as he listened to the message. He closed the
phone, then hurled it against the mattress. "What the hell
are you doing, Beth!"

"What did she say?" Reed asked urgently, though he
could guess.

"She—it doesn't matter. It's personal. But . . . I need to
get out of here. Find her."

"I'm coming with you."

"Whatever." Adam grabbed his jacket and his room
key, opened the door, then doubled back to slip into his
sneakers. Reed waited impatiently in the hallway, but Adam
paused, just before stepping through the threshold. "You
don't think she . . . I mean, she wouldn't . . ."

Reed was trying not to think at all. "Let's just find her,"
he suggested, striding down the hallway without waiting to
see if Adam would follow. "Soon."

"You want the truth? Fine. Truth."

Beth dug her fingers into the pitted stone of the gargoyle and tried not to shut her eyes against the stinging

wind. She wanted to see everything, even if it hurt.

"The truth is, I hate you," Harper shouted down.

Big surprise there.

"I've always hated you. You're weak, you're bland, you're spineless, you act like you're this model of virtue who always does the right thing, as if you get to look down on the rest of us because you never make any mistakes. Everything about you is a lie."

"Is this supposed to be helping?" Beth could feel the loose gravel between her left foot and wondered how big a gust of wind would be required to push her off balance. At least that way she wouldn't have to do it herself.

This was humiliating. She'd lowered herself down here, she'd made peace with her decision, and then—she'd frozen. Unwilling to go back up, unable to let herself go down, she'd stood in this gusty limbo for what felt like hours—until Harper arrived, apparently determined to ship her straight to hell.

"Why should I help you, after what you did to me? And to *her*?"

"You shouldn't!" Beth cried, her voice carried away on the wind, so that she didn't know whether or not she would even be heard. "No one should. That's the point."

"That's *my* point!" Harper shouted back. "Can't you come up with anything better than that? Can't you even defend yourself?"

"What am I supposed to say? I did it." After keeping it trapped inside all this time, it almost felt good to say it—to shout it—to know that when she did fall, it would be without secrets.

"You could say Kaia was a bitch who slept with your

boyfriend. You could say *I'm* a bitch who tried to ruin your life and drive you crazy—that I *did* drive you crazy, and you were just trying to get back at me. You could say you weren't the one who was driving the car."

Her perch was precarious, and she didn't dare look up again to see Harper's face. And Beth's imagination wasn't rich enough to come up with something that matched the odd mixture of rage, hysteria, and regret in her voice.

"I can't blame anyone else," Beth insisted. "I did it. I killed her. And this is the only way to make things right . . . even."

"Maybe you don't get to just blame yourself!" Harper yelled. "Maybe you don't get to decide who's guilty."

"So I'm supposed to blame you? For almost getting yourself killed? You want to join me down here?"

"You'd like that, wouldn't you? Because that would make everything neat and even again, right? Because you can't stand a fucking mess."

"I can't stand—"

"You can't stand to face it. To *deal* with it. You think you're doing the right thing? You're just doing what you always do, taking the easy way out. Look, you did something horrible. And maybe I . . ."

Now Beth did look up, just enough to see Harper leaning over the wall, her hair flying across her face, close enough to touch.

"I did something horrible too," Harper concluded. "But that doesn't mean, that *can't* mean—this. Kaia's dead. But we're not, and—"

"And that's not fair!" Beth screamed.

"Oh, grow up! Life isn't fair, you're not perfect, everything sucks—get the hell over it."

Beth wanted to believe her. She wanted to relieve her burden, hand out the blame like a pile of Christmas presents, climb back up onto the roof, go inside the hotel, and go on with the rest of her life as if nothing had ever happened. But . . .

"Harper, I don't know if I can."

The hallways were choked with clumps of drunken Haven seniors, talking, smoking, drinking, and grabbing at Adam as he pushed past. Everyone wanted something from him, and he just wanted to get away. He threaded his way through the crowd, tuning out the chatter and ignoring the gossip until one line finally penetrated:

"Dude, did you hear? There's some crazy chick up on the roof and it looks like she might jump!"

It felt like a pair of iron hands had wrapped around his throat and started to squeeze.

Nothing to do with me, he assured himself. *No one I know.* But as a flood of people crowded toward the elevators, he shoved them all out of the way, hurtling down the hall in the opposite direction, searching for Reed, knowing that he shouldn't waste the time but not wanting to go up there and face whatever there was to face alone.

And Reed deserved to know.

Adam found him, and without explanation—and maybe no explanation was needed, because maybe they had already known—they bypassed the clogged elevators and raced up the stairs, flight after flight, panting but never flagging, Adam several lengths ahead but pausing when he reached the top. They passed through the door together. A crowd of witnesses clustered in front of the door, hushed but disengaged, like they were watching it all unfold on reality TV. Adam knew he should push his way through the crowd, but he couldn't help it. He hesitated.

Beside him, Reed hadn't moved either.

All they had now were their fears—and a little hope. But when they saw what was really going on, there would be no more space for either. There would only be reality. And Adam wasn't ready to face it. Not yet.

"Beth, listen to me," Harper insisted with a new urgency, realizing somehow that this conversation—though it seemed too civilized a term for whatever was going on between them—was nearing its end, one way or another. "Maybe I started this, maybe you did, it doesn't matter— the point is, this can't be how this is supposed to end."

This. If she were stronger, maybe she could be clearer. *This never-ending nightmare of hatred and revenge and misery and death.*

And if she were bolder, maybe she could be more accurate. *I started it. You can't be the one to finish it.*

"You hate me," Beth whined. "I don't know why you even want . . . why you even care—"

"You hate me too," Harper pointed out. "You hated Kaia. But it didn't mean you wanted her—"

"No. No! I didn't want that. I never meant for it to happen. I swear. I promise. It just . . ."

"Happened. I know." And she wasn't just saying it. She could still hate Beth, blame Beth; she could still blame herself. She did. But—

That was the thing. There were no *but*s. No excuses. No explanations. No apologies that could ever be enough.

No way to make things right again, no way to make things even. And trying to do that, trying to go backward, reliving the moment over and over again, trying to justify and understand and escape the guilt—it didn't work. It left you on a ledge, twenty stories up, staring down at an empty parking lot, working up the courage to die.

There was no going backward, only forward. There could be no forgiveness, only acceptance. *This* had happened. And that wasn't going to change. So it was either live with the consequences, bear the guilt, and keep going—or the ledge. The parking lot. The other choice.

"This won't fix anything, Beth. This won't make anything even. You're not making up for what you did—you're just running away."

"So what am I supposed to do?"

"Stay. Fight. Feel guilty. Feel miserable. Hate me. Hate yourself. *Live.*" Harper hesitated. She had never told anyone what it was like, how bad it got at night, when she felt trapped inside her own body, when she wanted to punish herself, tear her own skin away or just crawl into a dark corner in the back of her mind, disappear into oblivion. But maybe Beth already knew. "It's impossible. Painful. And sometimes you . . . *I* just want it to fucking end. But I . . ."

"You what?"

"I keep going. I make it through a day, and then I make it through the next one. I don't give up. I try."

"What if I can't?" Beth's voice was almost too quiet to hear. Maybe it was the wind. "What if I'm not as . . . strong as you? What if I just can't?"

Harper paused, but it was too late for lies; there'd been too much truth. "Then I guess you give up," she said bitterly. "I guess you quit. You jump. But don't pretend that's some twisted kind of justice. Don't tell yourself that you're doing the right thing. Just . . . please. Don't."

He had expected to recognize the figure on the edge, he had expected the terror and the shock and the nausea. But he hadn't expected this.

"Harper?"

The night folded in on itself and, as if the last several nightmarish hours had never happened, he imagined for a moment that he was on a different roof, alone, and Harper was still waiting for him.

I never gave up on you, he told her silently. *On us.*

He had been so certain of his decision, so eager to find her, hold her, start all over again with a perfect kiss that would heal all their wounds. And then—circumstances had gotten in the way.

Apparently she wasn't waiting for him anymore. Apparently, she'd given up.

Before he could move, Harper had swung herself half over the wall. He opened his mouth to scream, but only a hoarse moan dribbled out, like he was in a dream. And it felt like a dream, everything moving so slowly, yet inexorably, toward a point he could see so vividly, it felt like it had already happened, and there was nothing he could do.

"No," he begged, but only in a whisper.

And then he saw a hand clasping Harper's, and a blond head emerging over the wall. From this distance he couldn't see her face, but he could picture the limpid blue eyes, and he could imagine the tears. Harper clutched her hand, pulled her over the wall, and back to safety. They stood there frozen for a moment, silhouetted against the neon skyline, holding hands like two paper dolls, in peril of blowing away. And then their hands dropped. Beth took a step forward, then another, and collapsed to the ground, shaking, her sobs echoing across the night.

Adam gave himself a moment to let the relief sink in, a moment of joy. And then he began to run.

It had all happened too fast, over before Reed even understood what was at stake, and what he'd almost lost. He'd seen her hair, her pale skin almost gleaming, and just like that, she'd been back on solid ground. And she needed him.

I loved you, he thought.

I hate you.

She'd taken Kaia away from him. She'd taken everything away, not just Kaia, but herself. She had been too good for him, too much for him, but she had loved him, and it had made the world glow—and it had all been a lie.

And yet.

She was still here. He had almost lost her, as he'd lost Kaia. But she was still here. Alive. Needing him. Maybe she wasn't the person he'd thought she was. But maybe—and he hated himself for thinking it, because it was a betrayal, it was treason—maybe it didn't matter.

She was still Beth, and she was still alive.

Maybe it's not too late.

And then it was.

By the time he took a step forward, Adam was already halfway across the roof. By the time he took another, Adam had scooped her up in his arms. Adam had pressed her head against his shoulder. Adam had saved the day.

Reed knew she could see him, and he waited for her to push Adam aside. To walk across the roof and apologize one more time, to give him a chance to forgive—and maybe this time he could. But she held Adam tight, and buried her face in his shoulder.

I loved you, Reed thought as he backed away through the crowd, through the doorway, inside, away. *I could have loved you. I love you.*

He didn't know which it was.

He didn't know where he was going.

He didn't care.

She had stupidly thought he was coming for her.

Harper had stood against the wall, eyes shut, breaths coming in deep, erratic gasps as the tension leaked out of her. Her hand had tightened, as if she still held Beth, knowing what would happen if she let go, and how easy it would be. Knowing she never would. She had, after a moment, taken in the crowd hovering fearfully by the stairwell, and tried to collect her energy to decide what to tell them.

It was Beth's story—Beth's show—but Harper knew she would have to direct it herself. She would dole out the details. She would handle the spin. She would make sure no one ever knew the truth. Because she could—because she was still standing, and Beth was crumpled on the ground, waiting for rescue.

Harper had done enough.

And then she saw Adam, and knew he had finally come for her. It was the wrong roof, the wrong time, but he was here, and she was ready. She'd meant what she'd told Beth, about forgiveness, about moving forward—now that he was here, she was ready to start again.

He had run toward her, and it seemed to take forever, his movements in slow motion, like the hero's run through a meadow in a cheesy movie, except that it didn't seem cheesy to Harper, it just seemed romantic. Perfect.

And then she realized she was in the wrong movie. She wasn't the heroine, and this wasn't her happy ending.

She was a cameo role, a plot device.

He swept Beth into his arms and she hung limp against him, her body curled up in his embrace.

Harper remembered telling Beth to get a spine, and realized it would be a useless purchase: She already had everything she needed to hold herself up. Adam hugged her, and rubbed her back, and from where she was standing, Harper could see her trembling, could hear her sobs.

Harper, on the other hand, held herself perfectly still. She forced herself to breathe evenly. She forced her eyes not to tear—she'd had plenty of practice.

And by the time Adam thought to look over at her, Beth's slim body draped across his chest, her hair spilling down his arm, Harper knew she had attained just the right look. The look that said, with ferocious determination, *I don't care.*

It all fell away as soon as she met his eyes. They looked haunted. She felt the tears spring into her own, and she was glad for the wall behind her, holding her upright. He gave her a half smile, one she recognized from years of friendship, the one he'd pulled out when he broke her Barbie doll or mashed a snowball into her face and given her a bloody nose. It said, *I'm sorry. I didn't mean to. I wish it had happened another way.*

He opened his mouth, as if to speak. But they had known each other for so long, they didn't need words.

She could, if she allowed herself, read the truth in his face. Whatever it was.

She needs me now, but I need you. Just wait.

Or maybe:

I choose her. Again.

Harper, he mouthed silently. *Please.*

She could know everything, if she wanted to. Just from watching his face, looking in his eyes. But whatever he had to say to her, it wouldn't change the fact that his arms were still wrapped around Beth. That Harper stood off to the side, watching, alone.

She might need to wait a lifetime, or maybe just a day.

But she was Harper Grace, and she was tired of waiting. He'd made his choice. Now it was her turn.

And she turned away.

chapter

14

Home.

It was a six-hour drive, without traffic. Time he needed, to think. To figure things out. But he was having some trouble with that.

The thinking.

It was all muddled in his brain, the last twenty-four hours, the fear and the relief and the regret all bleeding together into a muddy, impenetrable sludge. Adam clenched the wheel tightly. He'd driven Kane's car plenty of times before, but never without Kane in the passenger's seat, hounding him to speed up, warning him of the penalties of living life in the slow lane—and the even graver penalties of denting Kane's Camaro.

But Kane was riding home in Miranda's car, with Harper. Where Adam was no longer welcome.

It was easy to zone out, to listen to the gravel under the wheels and the wind against the dash. It was easy to pretend that by the time he got home, everything that had happened would be forgotten. Life would return to normal.

But he knew it was a lie. Harper wouldn't forgive him, not this time—at least, not unless he was willing to meet her demands. And he couldn't. He had responsibilities now, and he couldn't walk away, even if it meant losing—

No. He wouldn't think about that. He couldn't afford to. Not when Beth sat beside him, her eyes closed, her face still stained with tears. What he wanted, what he'd lost, it wasn't important now. Beth was the one in trouble—and someone had to make sure that, whatever happened, she never ended up on that roof again. She was weak, in need. He was strong, and he could be there for her.

He *would*.

He was glad she'd finally fallen asleep in the passenger's seat, glad she felt comfortable enough—safe enough—to close her eyes and escape from everything, at least for a few hours. If only he could do the same.

Love.

Was it possible? *I'm in love,* Miranda thought, pretending she was saying it casually, the way you'd say, *I have a toothache* or *I'm hungry.* Like it was something that happened to you all the time. Like it wasn't something you'd been dreaming of for years, all the while forcing yourself to stop, knowing that you had no chance of ever getting the thing you most desperately wanted.

I got it, though. She turned toward Kane, who took his eyes off the road just long enough to give her a warm smile. *I got* him.

She knew she needed to slow down. She wasn't in

love—or, at least, *he* wasn't in love, not yet, and until both people felt the same way, it didn't count. She knew that better than anyone, since she was the one who'd been longing, for all these years, watching him from a distance, waiting for him to notice.

She still didn't understand why he suddenly had.

She should be cautious. She understood that. He hadn't made her any promises, hadn't talked about the future. Yes, he had implied that there was now *something* where there had been nothing, but they were on vacation. It was Vegas, where anything goes. What would he want from her when they got back home? What if he didn't want anything?

But her doubts couldn't make much of a dent in her happiness. Not even Harper, moody and silent in the backseat, could do that. Miranda had already forgiven her best friend—in the mood she was in, she would have forgiven anyone anything—but much as she wanted to, she couldn't force herself to wallow in Harper's misery. She didn't have room for it in her brain.

Her body glowed with the memory of Kane's touch, and she touched him now, just because she could. His hand rested on the gearshift, and, still a little terrified, she wrapped hers around it. He smiled at her again.

She was allowed to touch him now, whenever she wanted. She was allowed to kiss him. Maybe she was even allowed to fall in love with him.

Miranda wasn't stupid. She knew she was getting ahead of herself, that things were too new, too uncertain, that if she let herself go too far too fast, she could end up getting hurt.

But with their hands pressed together, none of that

seemed to matter. When Kane smiled at her—with that look in his eye, the one she'd always been waiting for, the one that said *I want* you—she couldn't help it.

She felt like she would never hurt again.

Maybe.

That's what Kane kept telling himself. He didn't *know* it was a bad decision; he wasn't *sure* it was going to lead to disaster. Yes, there was that feeling in his gut, that *Oh, shit* feeling that had never steered him wrong before. But backing down just because he expected disaster? That would be giving in to fear. And that was unacceptable.

She kept darting glances at him, nervous, adoring looks. *Smile back,* he instructed himself. *Play along.*

Except that he wasn't playing, not this time—and that was the problem.

Miranda was the one he should be worried about. She was fragile, even if she pretended not to be. He knew he could hurt her—he knew exactly how to do it. And this whole thing, this ludicrously bad idea he'd had, it was probably a good way to start.

And yet . . .

Maybe it was a worthwhile experiment. That's how he would look at it: an experiment. Nothing less, nothing more. Maybe he could let someone in, maybe she really was different from the rest of them, the girls he strung along until they got too close, or he got too bored.

It's not like he had proposed or anything. A kiss was not a promise. A beginning didn't have to last forever.

Stop making such a big deal out of this, he thought, focusing on the road. He wouldn't look at her again, not for a while. He would concentrate on the road ahead of them, on the wide, cement path stretching to the horizon. He would clear his mind and analyze his options. He would *not* panic.

And by the time they got back home, maybe he would have an answer. He would have figured out how to make this thing work—or, at least, whether he wanted to try. *What happens in Vegas* . . . he reminded himself. It could be a mistake, trying to bring a piece of the city home with them. The two of them together, it had made sense back there—but that was a foreign land. A million miles away from Grace, CA. Who knew what would happen when they tried to fit themselves back into their old lives—together.

It could work, he decided, feeling her watching him again.

Maybe.

Empty.

It was as if someone had carved out her insides and dumped them in the garbage. Or maybe they were leaking out, slowly but steadily, because the farther away they got from Vegas, the emptier Harper felt. It was as if she'd left behind everything that had ever mattered to her, and part of her wanted to scream at Kane, beg him to stop the car, turn around, take her back.

But a U-turn wouldn't help—what she needed was a time machine.

It was so strange, being back in the car again, back on the same highway, as if nothing had changed, when everything had. She was in the backseat now, while Kane and Miranda sat together in the front, not talking, just exchanging sly little glances, speaking to each other in that silent language that all couples have. The wordless communion that left everyone else out in the cold. Harper wanted to be happy for them, but she didn't have it in her. All she could see was the potential for pain; all she could believe was that, in the end, everyone ended up alone.

She had been so optimistic on the way to Vegas, stupidly thinking that she could find happiness there, that Sin City would somehow show her a way to wash herself of her sins.

They say you can find anything in Vegas, but all she'd found were answers. She knew whom to blame now. She knew who was on her side—and who wasn't.

Harper stared out the window, out at the desert flatness, remembering how much Kaia had hated the unchanging scenery, with its dusty infinities and scraggly brush, as if the land had a skin condition. The ground was pitted and pockmarked. Diseased.

She closed her eyes, trying to regain the certainty she'd felt up on that roof, her belief in the necessity of moving forward. And maybe it was possible. They had hours left on the road, time enough to cleanse herself. She would leave her emotional baggage in Vegas, and arrive back in Grace refreshed and renewed.

She would leave behind the anger, the pain of betrayal, the misguided hope, the guilt, the bitterness. And, hardest of all, most important of all, she would leave behind the love. She would leave Adam; she would stop clinging to the past and stop hoping they could go back.

But if she succeeded, if she really could leave it all behind . . . what would she have left?

Lost.

"Shit!" Reed pounded the wheel in frustration. He'd just passed the same crappy Howard Johnson for the third time in a row. Confirmation that he was no closer to the highway entrance than he'd been an hour ago. A fucking waste of time, just like the entire weekend, he thought.

Except not a total waste—at least he'd found out the truth. That was something.

He cursed the guys for ditching him—they'd hooked up with a couple of Haven High's hottest stoner girls and were staying in town an extra night. How was he supposed to read the map and drive at the same time without crashing into the side of the damn Howard Johnson?

Maybe it wouldn't be the worst thing in the world, he thought.

Then hated himself for thinking it.

He pulled the van into a gas station, intending to ask for directions. But instead of getting out, he just sat there, resting his head against the cool leather steering wheel. Then he lit a joint and let his mind drift.

Maybe this was a sign. Maybe he was supposed to be lost, stranded in Vegas, hundreds of miles from home. It wasn't much of a home, not now, after Kaia . . . after Beth.

He'd gambled and he'd lost. Big. He'd lost it all. He could start over again in Vegas. Wait tables, get a cheap apartment, start up a new band. Track down Star★la. He could make a new life for himself.

He knew it wasn't realistic. It wasn't going to happen. But it was nice to imagine, just for a while. It was nice to ignore the future, the crap he would face when he got back to Grace, the pain that would slice through the fog as soon as the buzz wore off.

Eventually, he'd go inside, get directions, hit the highway, drive home. He just didn't know why. He'd lost it all this weekend, so what did he have to go back for?

Nothing.

Hope.

Beth had thought she would never experience it again. And maybe you couldn't call it hope yet, not quite. It was just a tiny kernel of an emotion, buried so far down that she wouldn't have known it was there if she hadn't been so raw, if everything she thought or felt hadn't screamed for attention. There was still so much pain, fear, sorrow, and, as always, guilt—but now there was something else, too. A tiny bright spot, a fresh breath. An expectation that maybe, just maybe, the worst was behind her.

Hope.

Her terrible secret had come out, she had been exposed—and then accused, and then abandoned. But not completely. She squeezed her hand into a fist, remembering how tightly Harper had grabbed her, how Beth hadn't wanted to let go. Harper wanted her to live.

And, as she had realized on that roof, staring down at the cement, willing herself to take the step, Beth wanted it too.

Adam hadn't spoken, not since they'd gotten onto the highway. And Beth didn't know what to say, so eventually she had closed her eyes and pretended to sleep. She didn't know what was going to happen next, when they got home, when she had to face Harper again. When she had to face the absence of Reed, who she knew would never come back to her.

Adam, she thought. *Remember Adam.* She could hear him breathing next to her. She could smell his familiar, comfortable scent, and knew that if she put her hand on his, he wouldn't pull away. He wasn't repulsed by her. He didn't hate her. He wanted to help—he wanted to forgive.

He didn't think she was worthless. And that was a start.

It seemed silly to hope, to think that anything good could happen or that her life could return to some kind of even balance, something tolerable, not weighed down by guilt and misery. But she couldn't help it. Behind her, Vegas was dipping beneath the horizon, and it felt like all the horrible things she'd done—or, at least, that one horrible thing she'd done—was receding along with it.

Maybe Harper had been right.

Beth didn't deserve happiness, forgiveness, or peace.

But maybe somehow she would find them anyway.

Here's a taste of the next—and last—*sinful* read . . .

Greed

The coach stood up. "This is him, our star."

The man sitting across from Coach Wilson stood up and grasped Adam's hand, pumping it up and down. "A pleasure," he said. "The coach was showing me some game tapes, and that shot you got off in the playoffs? Remarkable."

"Uh . . . thanks," Adam said, shooting a helpless look at his coach. When was somebody going to tell him what was going on?

"And your foul-shot ratio is damn impressive," the guy continued, "though we may have to work on your shooting stance—it's a little loose, but that's easily fixed with the proper training. No offense, coach," he said, turning toward Coach Wilson, who'd settled back into the guidance counselor's chair.

"Hey, you're the expert," the coach said, grinning. "I'm just a lil' old high school coach. What do I know?"

"Enough to beat me eleven-three last time we played," the guy pointed out.

"Oh, that's right!" The coach slapped his forehead in exaggerated surprise. "I forgot all about that."

"Bullshit. It's all I heard about for a month."

"Uh, Coach?" Adam said hesitantly. He nodded toward the clock. "My next class is going to start soon, and—"

"Where are my manners?" the guy said, indicating that Adam should take a seat. "The name's Brian Foley. Your coach and I went to high school together, back in the Stone Age."

"Brian's a coach now at UC Riverside," his coach said, giving Adam a look that was obviously supposed to be meaningful; Adam just didn't know what it was supposed to mean.

"Here's the deal, Adam," the UC guy said. "I've got a last-minute spot on next year's squad, and I want you." He tossed Adam a white and yellow T-shirt reading UCR HIGHLANDERS. "You've got Highlander written all over you."

"Me? But—I didn't even apply to Riverside," Adam said. "I'm going to State, in Borrega."

"Do they even have a basketball team?" the UC coach asked in disdain. "Listen to what I'm telling you, Adam. I *want* you on my team. And I can *get* you on my team. Doesn't matter if you applied to the school or not. I've seen your transcripts, I can get you admitted. I think I can even manage a scholarship. It'll take some doing, but . . . I've seen you play, and you're the guy to play for me."

"You can really do all that?" Adam asked, trying to process. He was going to the state school in Borrega; that had always been the plan. It was an hour away from home, one step up from community college, and everyone he knew would be there, too. Harper would be there.

"Adam, my friend, welcome to the wonderful world of

college athletics." Coach Foley stretched back in his seat. "I can do pretty much anything I want. And, once you're a Highlander, so can you."

Adam squirmed under the guy's fiercely confident stare. "I don't know . . ." He'd been counting the days until he could finally get out of school and never come back. Moving hundreds of miles away to some strange place where he wouldn't know anyone, and would need to work even harder than he had in high school? What was the point? "School's not really my thing."

"Morgan, be smart," Coach Wilson said. "This is your shot—UC Riverside's got a great team and, more than that, you'll get a degree that's actually worth something. And, once Brian here works his magic, you'll practically get it for free. This is what we in the coaching biz like to call a 'win-win situation.' Don't pass it up."

"He doesn't have to decide right now," the UC coach said, standing up. He leaned over and shook Adam's hand again. "You've got two weeks." He handed Adam a business card. Adam stared down at it, stunned, still expecting the whole thing to be a joke. But the card looked real. And both coaches looked dead serious. "Call me by June fourteenth, if you're interested. Otherwise, the spot goes to someone else."

Beth flipped through the empty pages of her yearbook, trying not to care. There were a few signatures, all variations on a theme:

It was fun being in _____ *class with you. Good luck in college next year—not that you need it!*

Whenever Beth was asked to sign a yearbook—and it

didn't happen often—she scanned the other entries, comparing them to the ones in her own. They referenced wild nights and inside jokes, testified to years of friendship, and bemoaned the end of an era. But Beth didn't get any of that. No, she just got *Have a great summer!*

There was only one section whose pages were filled with cramped handwriting and messages of enthusiastic sincerity. But that was more of an embarrassment than a triumph. Lucky for Beth, no one ever bothered to search through her yearbook, counting up her signatures, so there was no one to notice that after four years of high school, her only true friends were her teachers.

"I'm really going to miss you," Ms. Polansky said, signing her entry with a flourish.

"I'll miss you, too," Beth told her junior year English teacher, wishing she could slip back in time. Things had been easy when she was a junior; *life* had been easy.

"Oh, I doubt it," the teacher said, laughing. The rare smile made her look several years younger. Although Beth knew that Ms. Polansky had been intimidating Haven High students ever since her parents were in school, she sometimes had trouble believing that the lithe, impeccably tailored woman in front of her was well into her sixties. Maybe all that snapping and eraser-throwing kept a person young; it certainly kept her students alert. "Once you get to Berkeley, you'll forget all about us—you'll get a chance to see what *real* teaching is like."

Beth flushed and dipped her head, letting her blond hair fall over her eyes. "I, um, didn't get into Berkeley," she admitted to the woman who'd written her a rave recommendation for her dream school.

Ms. Polansky pursed her lips, then gave a sharp nod. "No matter, no matter," she said briskly. "Plenty of good schools, and students like you can excel anywhere. If I remember, your second choice was . . . UCLA?"

Beth rubbed her hand against the back of her neck and made a small noise of agreement. She glanced over her shoulder at the door, wishing there was some graceful way she could cut short the conversation and flee. Anything not to have to admit the truth and see the look on her favorite teacher's face. Telling her parents had been difficult enough. This would be unbearable.

"And you were accepted, I presume?"

Beth made another noncommittal noise.

"What's that?" Ms. Polansky asked sharply.

"Yes," Beth said, sighing heavily. "I got in."

"Buck up," the teacher told her. "I spent some time in L.A. as a young woman—many, many years ago, as you can imagine—and it's really quite the exotic locale. I'm sure someone like you will have no trouble—"

"I'm not going," Beth admitted, ripping it off fast, like a Band-Aid. But it still hurt.

"What's that?"

Beth settled into one of the chairs in the front row of the empty classroom, feeling a strange sense of déjà vu, as if any minute Ms. Polansky would start lecturing about MacBeth's motivations in the third act while Beth struggled not to think about whether Adam would like her dress for the junior prom.

"Some stuff happened this year, and, uh, I turned down my acceptance," Beth said. She didn't say the part about how she'd thought there was no point to planning a future when she couldn't imagine living through the next day, or the next. Nor did she mention that she had expected to spend next year lying on a couch with her stoner boyfriend, choking on a cloud of pot that would help her forget everything she was passing up.

"Why would you do a stupid thing like that?" Ms. Polansky snapped.

Beth winced. She had always loved the teacher's bluntness and her high expectations—but that was back when she could meet them. "I'm just stupid, I guess."

"You're the farthest thing from that." Ms. Polansky settled down at the desk next to her. Her voice softened. "What happened?"

Beth shrugged. "I made a mistake."

"Can you fix it?"

"No." Not that she hadn't tried. Her father had tried. Her guidance counselor had tried. But it was permanent; it was over. "I missed the deadline. They'd still be willing to let me in, but . . . I lost my scholarship. And without it . . ." Beth shrugged again. Without the money, there was no way. She'd always known that. It was the reason she'd worked so hard every day, every year, knowing that her only shot for the future was in being perfect. And she'd actually managed it, right up until the very end, when she'd thrown it all away. "I'm thinking about taking some night classes . . . community college or something. . . ."

Ms. Polansky handed the yearbook back to her and stood up. "Well then. That's settled. I'm sure you'll find a way to make it work."

"I'm sorry," Beth said.

"For what?"

"For . . . letting you down."

"Nonsense," the teacher said. "You're only letting yourself down."

Beth realized it was true. And that was even worse.

"For old time's sake?" Miranda had begged, launching into a long guilt trip about how they didn't spend enough time together anymore, and how everything was about to change, and all she was asking was this one tiny thing. . . .

Eventually Harper had agreed, just to shut her up.

She stuffed a limp, greasy fry in her mouth, washing it down with a swig of flat Diet Coke. "Exactly which part of this are you going to miss?" she asked Miranda, who was gazing at the tacky fluorescent décor like it was the Sistine Chapel.

Miranda squeezed closer to Kane, who was stroking her arm with one hand and stealing fries off her untouched plate with the other. "This," Miranda insisted. *"Us."*

"I see you every day, Rand," Harper pointed out. "And next year, when we get the hell out of here and get our own apartment, I'll see you even more. And as for your boyfriend, here," she jerked her head at Kane, "I could do with seeing him a little less."

"You know you'll miss me next year," Kane said, flashing her a smug grin. "What would you do without me?"

"Ce-le-brate good times," Harper sang tunelessly.

"Your life would be dull and colorless without me," Kane argued.

"Oh, Geary, I know how much you love to be right, so why don't you prove it? You leave and never come back, and I'll e-mail you to let you know how it all turns out."

Kane grabbed a straw from the table, tore off one end of the wrapper, then brought the straw to his lips and blew the wrapper into Harper's face. "Patience, Grace. All good things come to those who wait."

Harper grinned—then spotted the hint of a quiver in Miranda's lower lip. *Stupid*, she told herself. Miranda had been dreaming about Kane for years, and now that she finally had him, he was headed east to college in less than three months. And Harper just *had* to dredge it up and turn it into a joke.

"I'll be waiting a long time," she said quickly. "Fall feels like forever away. *Graduation* feels like forever away."

"It's only two weeks," Miranda pointed out, picking at her salad. "And I just thought coming back here at least once before it's all over—it would be like the old days."

The Nifty Fifties diner, with its peeling movie posters and Buddy Holly tunes blasting out of the ancient juke-box, was the perfect spot for nostalgia. Especially since they'd been coming here several nights a week since ninth grade. The fab four: Harper, Kane, Miranda—and Adam.

Now Kane and Miranda were nuzzling each other and sharing a shake, while Harper sat on her side of the booth, alone. And Adam was . . . somewhere else.

"You're such a sap," Harper told her best friend.

"That's what you told me the first time we came here," Miranda said, beaming. "When I said I wished people still wore poodle skirts and went to drive-in movies and danced the Jitterbug."

Harper rolled her eyes. "You're also a freak—how do you remember *everything* that's ever happened?"

"I think it's cute," Kane said, giving her a peck on the cheek. Miranda blushed, and her smile grew wider. "Freakish, but cute."

"As long as you two are already in mockery mode," Miranda said, "now would probably be a good time for . . ." She pulled out her digital camera.

"No!" Harper said, waving her hands in front of her face. Miranda had been documenting everything that had happened for the last couple weeks, and enough was enough.

"No way," Kane said, trying to grab the camera out of Miranda's hands. She squirmed away. "No need to document another lame night in the world's lamest diner."

"Come on," Miranda begged. "For me?"

Kane looked at Harper. Harper rolled her eyes. "The things we do for love," she said, spreading her arms in defeat. She waved Kane over to her side of the booth. "Come on, let's get this over with."

Kane squeezed in next to her and they pressed their heads together. Miranda held up the camera. "Kane," she said reproachfully. "Don't do that."

"Is he holding up bunny ears behind my head?" Harper asked, jabbing him in the side.

"Not exactly. . . ."

Harper whirled around, but Kane was sitting calmly by her side, hands in his lap, angelic smile on his face, the picture of innocence. "Can we just take the picture?" he asked. "What's the holdup?"

Harper glared at him and turned back to the camera.

"Think happy thoughts," Miranda said cheerfully.

Harper thought about the first time they had come

here together: Kane complaining about the decorations, Miranda ordering two sundaes in a row, Adam whining about how his new girlfriend snorted when she laughed, and Harper breathing it all in, savoring the brief vacation from posing, performing, impressing, all the effort she put into maintaining her social position every second of every day. For a couple hours, she could just be with her friends, no worries, no fears, just overcooked burgers and soggy fries.

"Smile," Miranda said.

But as the camera flashed, Harper's mouth dropped open and her eyebrows knit together in alarm, turning her face into a fright mask of shock and horror. Because just before the camera flash had blinded her, she'd glanced toward the door. The perfect couple—blond, bronzed, beautiful—had just walked in. They weren't holding hands, but they were a couple nonetheless. Anyone could see it. Harper just didn't want to.

They were heading right for her.

"What's *he* doing here?" Harper spat.

Miranda turned around, then looked back at Harper, her eyes wide. "I don't know, I didn't—" She suddenly looked at Kane. "Did you?"

Kane tapped his fingers on the table. "I probably should have mentioned it sooner, but . . ."

"What were you thinking?" Miranda hissed.

"I was thinking *she* wasn't coming," he whispered, jerking his head toward Harper. "Like you told me."

"Then I told you she *was* coming."

"Well by then it was too late, wasn't it?"

"You could have said something," Miranda complained.

"I just did."

"Forget it," Harper snapped. "It doesn't matter. It's done. I'm out of here." She stood up, just as Adam and Beth reached the table. Beth was wearing a pale green polka-dotted sundress with a white sash around the waist that looked like it belonged at a post-golf garden party—but, fashion don't or not, it still showed off her long limbs and deep tan. *Lawn Party Barbie*, Harper thought in disgust. *And she's finally reclaimed her Ken.*

"Harper," Adam said in surprise. "I didn't know you were going to be here."

"I'm not," Harper said. "This is just an optical illusion. It'll be over in a second."

"You don't have to go just because—"

"Yes." She glared at Beth, who at least had the decency to look away. "I do."

Beth closed the car door and settled back into the passenger seat with a loud sigh of relief. "Well, that was . . ."

"Awkward." Adam stuck the key into the ignition, trying not to replay the night in his mind. It had been a mistake to bring Beth; it had been a mistake to come in the first place. It had, mostly, been a mistake to think that he could make things normal again just by wishing it.

"Awkward with a capital *A*," Beth agreed.

"I'm sorry."

"No, *I'm* sorry. You warned me that Kane was going to be there, and . . ."

"I didn't know about Harper or—" Adam pulled out of the lot, reminded of all the nights he'd come to the diner to pick Beth up after her shift. Back when she still worked there; back when they were still in love.

"Please don't apologize," she said. "They're your friends. You should get to hang out with them. And I . . . I should have been smart enough to stay home where I belong."

"No." He reached over to squeeze her shoulder. "You're my friend, too. And if they can't handle that . . ." No one had said so out loud, of course. Beth and Kane had snipped at each other, Miranda, loyal to the bitter end, had glared silently down at the table, unwilling to engage the enemy—Harper's enemy. And Adam had tried to keep up a nonstop stream of meaningless conversation without calling attention to the fact that everyone around him was miserable. It would have been hard enough under normal circumstances, but tonight, still shaken from his encounter with the UC Riverside coach, Adam wasn't quite at his best. He hadn't told anyone about the offer; he still wasn't sure he believed it. And he didn't know what it would do to Beth if he left.

"I know," she said quietly. "Thank you."

"Please stop thanking me. I'm not doing you a favor by hanging out with you. I care about you."

He laid his hand over hers, and she squeezed it. "It means a lot that you're always there for me."

Not always, he thought, self-hatred rising like bile. *Not when you needed me.*

An old Simon and Garfunkel song came on the radio, and Adam turned it up.

"I love this song," Beth said, smiling faintly.

"I remember."

"Reed always used to make fun of me for liking this kind of stuff but . . . sorry."

He glanced over at her, then back at the road. "What?"

"I shouldn't talk about him, with you. I mean, it's kind of weird, right?"

Adam shrugged. "A lot of stuff is weird right now," he pointed out. "You should talk about him. If you want."

"I don't."

They listened to the music. Beth sang along under her breath. Her voice was a little thin, but sweet and on-key, just as he remembered.

"Okay," he said eventually, pulling the car up to the curb in front of her house. "Door-to-door service, as requested."

"Thanks for—you know . . . thanks," she muttered, fumbling with her seatbelt and scooping her bag off the floor.

Adam turned the car off. "Beth, wait." Before, when they were together, she had always pushed him to think about the future. She had wanted better for him than the life he'd planned for himself. And she had always given him the best advice. "Something kind of weird happened this morning, and uh . . . can I ask you something?"

"Anything." She tucked a strand of hair behind her ear. Adam had always loved it when she wore it down like this, cascading over her shoulders. He liked to run his hands through it and breathe in its fruity scent.

"I got called down to the guidance office," he began hesitantly, "and there was this guy there, with the coach . . ."

She nodded, waiting for him to continue.

But he couldn't. She was depending on him. He could see it in her face. She needed him. If he was going to leave, he would have to tell her in the right way, at the right time, and this wasn't it. He couldn't say anything, not until he'd made his decision. Then he could figure out how to go, without hurting her.

"Never mind," he said.

"What? You can tell me."

"No, it's just some stupid basketball thing. It's no big deal. So, I guess, have a good night, okay?"

"Ad, I know you don't want me to thank you any more, but—" Beth leaned across the seat and gave him a tight hug. He rested his chin on her shoulder and listened to her breathing. "I owe you," she whispered. "For everything."

She let go, but he held on, pulling away only enough to see her face. It was mostly hidden in shadow. There was a tear clinging to the corner of her left eye. She gave him a half smile. "Déjà vu, right?"

He knew that she was thinking of all the nights he'd dropped her off at home, lingering in the car for one last kiss, before the living room lights flicked on, her mother's signal that it was time to go inside.

"A lot's changed," he said softly. "But . . ."

"It still feels kind of . . ."

"Yeah."

You couldn't put it into words, the feeling between them, that comfort of knowing the other person, of having been through the pain and the lies and the guilt and coming out the other side.

Beth's face was a portrait of sorrow. He could almost see the old woman she would become someday, the worry lines and creases, the sagging of time weighing her down. She wasn't the same girl he'd been in love with. If he'd even been in love. She was watching him, like she was waiting for something.

So he kissed her.

It was light, it was hesitant, and then, almost as quickly, it was over.

She pulled away from him, but not in anger. Just surprise. "What was—?"

"I don't know," Adam said quickly. "I just thought . . ."

"You mean you want to . . . ?"

"I don't know." Adam looked down at his hands. One of them was resting next to hers, and he inched it over until their pinkies were interlocked, just like he always used to. "Do you?"